Killer

by DW Beam

Published in the USA in 2018 by
DW Beam Publishing,
King, NC

ISBN: 978-1-943-455-17-1

Cover Design by DW Beam
Edited by DW Beam Publishing

This book is a fictional work. Any resemblance to actual people,
places, or events is unintentional. This book is not intended for
children or a young audience.

Author's email: dwbeam@dwbeampublishing.com

Chapter 1
Respect

There is a knock on the door. I know who it is. I know what they want.

"Sheriff's Department. Open the door please."

I reach for the handle. I open it very slowly.

"Are you Mr.—"

"Yeah, I'm who you want. I'm guilty."

"Sir, you're under arrest. You will have to come with us."

It's the first time in a long time that I have seen real handcuffs, but not long enough. I didn't like 'em then, and I don't like 'em now. And I don't like my hands behind my back. It's my shoulder. I hurt it when I was younger, and I hurt it again not too long ago.

"Can you put the handcuffs in front, Deputy?"

"I'm afraid not."

I say, "You don't understand, Deputy. I can't sit in the car like this. My shoulder's messed up."

"I'm afraid there's nothing I can do about that."

Well, I tried, but as soon as I'm put in the car, it isn't 'til they drive off that things get a little dark. You see, when I lean back on that seat, it pushes up on my shoulder. I get a little sick at first, and then everything goes black.

I feel a tug on my shirt. "Alright, you, come on."

After a few short pants of breath, he pulls my feet around. "You better not kick me," the deputy sheriff says.

"What?"

"You heard me."

I'm confused at first when they get me to my feet.

After they get the handcuffs off of me, fingerprint me, and put me in a cell, here comes two other officers. "You need to come with us."

"What, no interrogation?"

He smiles at me. I smile back.

"We got a live one here," the other guy says.

I look at him and say, "Yeah, I'm alive."

"Yeah, you are," the deputy that arrested me says, "but the twelve people you murdered ain't."

"I didn't murder nobody. Let's get this straight right now."

"What?!? But you said... Oh never mind, you just get on in there.

"What's this?" I ask, looking at the papers on the table.

"These are forms," the sheriff says.

"What are they for?" I ask, playing along, of course. I know what they are for. They are confession forms.

Twelve of 'em.

Twelve signatures.

Twelve deaths.

The first one I come to, shot three times in the heart.

"So you want me to confess to this?"

"Why not? You did it."

"What if I didn't do it? What if I saw one of your goons do it?"

"That's highly unlikely," the sheriff says. "Most of these goons you're talking about or referring to— which I find offensive by the way— they weren't even sheriffs or deputy sheriffs when you committed this murder."

———————

It was my first kill. It was late afternoon. Here he came out of an executive building. I knew exactly what he was doing, but I didn't care. It was a .357. I opened the cylinder up, spun it around, looked at the bullets, and closed it back up.

He got into his big fancy car and began to drive off. It was where he stopped.

A big fancy house.

Rich people.

I couldn't stand it.

He had to be stopped.

I didn't like him, and I knew he didn't like me.

He walked onto the porch. I had been practicing the triple credit card trick for years, and now it would pay off. Take three or four credit cards and put 'em together. When he unlocked the door and went in, I ran up and put the credit cards inside the lip to where the door wouldn't shut all the way.

I grabbed the handle. Now the door was locked on the other side. As he checked it and pulled it a little bit, I held it still. When he let go of the handle, I waited a few moments. After a few minutes, I pushed the door open just a little, and then I sat down on the porch there.

It was a long while, but then came what I was waiting on. The living room lights went out. I stepped out into the yard. There it was. The light in the bedroom window. I stepped into the door. It was dark at first, but after I got all the way in, I shut the door back quickly.

I walked up to the bedroom. The light was on, so I went on in. There was no one there. I must have passed him by downstairs, or else I would have seen him. I turned around just in time. There he stood.

"It's you!" he yelled out as he looked down at the gun.

"Yes, it's me."

Three times right in the heart.

The first time I shot, it knocked him so hard he flew back against the wall on the other side of the hall. His head was shaking backward and forward really fast, looking at me. I pointed the gun at him again. Two more shots right beside the other one.

I had stalked him for weeks.

————————

The sheriff pulls out a .357. "You seen this before?"

"Yeah, I've seen it before. It's mine."

"That's an admission of guilt."

4

"No, it's not," I say abruptly. "Exactly what do you want from me?" I ask.

"The truth," he says. "Now sign the damn paper. You know you killed him. It's murder in the first degree."

"No, I won't sign it."

"What do you mean you won't sign it? You admit you killed him, right?"

"Yes, I killed him, and I'll sign a paper saying I killed him. But you got right here, murder in the first degree."

"So if I change the paperwork and take out murder and just put kill there, you'll sign it?"

"Sure."

"I'll be right back."

He picks up the .357 and the paperwork and stays gone for a long time. I haven't used the bathroom. I haven't had anything to drink, and I was a little hungry to start with. They had came to get me a little sooner than I expected. But now I'm just getting ill. After three hours, he comes back with a Sprite and a cup half the size of the can with a little ice in it.

"Is that for me?" I ask.

"After you sign the paper."

I say, "Sheriff, you better be a little nicer to me if you want me to be more cooperative. Now are you gonna give me the drink or not?"

He slides it toward me at the same time he slides the first paperwork.

The first words, I hereby confess that I shot and killed such and such person at such and such time on such and such day. I put my signature at the bottom of the paper.

A big smile comes on his face. "Now we're getting somewhere. Now the next one."

_____

She was twenty years old. Everybody liked her. I've got to admit, I had trouble with this one. She was so nice to everybody. I followed her around for two weeks. Yeah, I stalked her. I knew where she went, what she did, what she ate, what she drank. I knew everything about her.

But that day, she left work. She stopped at a coffee shop. She never knew I was there. She giggled. She laughed. Everybody smiled. Everybody liked her.

She pulled up to a gas station. I couldn't hear what they were saying, but I could see the big smile on his face. He was so pleased to help her. Gas, he even cleaned her windows, smiling and talking the whole time.

But it didn't change my feelings.

She had to die.

She was beautiful, sitting in front of a mirror at a vanity. She never knew I was in the bedroom until she looked up into the mirror.

She said, "Oh no! Please don't kill me!" She was horrified at what she saw, but it wasn't what she saw that killed her. It was who she saw.

I shot her in the back of the head on the side. She melted to the floor. Then, I walked over, cold to the bone, and shot her three times in the chest.

"You read enough? You killed her. Sign the damn paper," the sheriff says.

"Not 'til you apologize for cursing at me, both times."

He pinches his lips together and looks at me cold and hard. "Afraid of a little curse word, killer?"

I sit there and look at the palm of my hand strapped to a table. Just long enough, well, to look at my palm and put my hand back down on the seat.

"What are you waiting for?" he asks.

"Respect," I answer.

"So you think you deserve respect? Look at her head!!!" He throws the pictures on the table. "This is murder in the first degree."

"You spent three hours while ago. I thought you changed all these papers." I pick 'em up and throw 'em at him. "Come back when you got 'em right, just like the first one. Otherwise, we're through talking."

When the papers hit him, he raises up his hand to strike me across the face. I hold my face up to let him strike. He pulls back with his anger intensified. But after I close my eyes and wait for a moment, I decide he must want me to see it coming, so I look at him. He still has his hand up, shaking his head.

"Respect. If you don't give me respect, I won't give it back to you," I tell him.

"Look Mr. Hourson—"

"Now we're getting somewhere, Mr. McDowell," I say.

He takes in a deep breath as he wipes his hand across his mouth and goes out the door. I fall asleep on the table and drool quite a puddle.

"Wake up, you! Respect, is it?" I wake up to him saying.

"That's right. Respect. I don't think it's too much to ask."

I begin to read the paper as he slides it across the table. "I hereby certify to the fact that I shot and killed..."

That's when I see her name written for the first time. It was the second name on my list. A list that was quite long. It has been ten long years since I killed her.

"So you do admit that you shot her and killed her, right?"

"Yes, I did. I shot her in the back of the head, and then I shot her three times in the heart."

He quivers when I say that. The fact is, I'm so cold and insensitive about it that it brings tears to his eyes. Fear enters into the room.

"Settle down, Sheriff. You've got nothing to fear from me. I would never hurt you."

He takes another breath. I sign the paper, slowly with anticipation. When I'm through, I slide the paper back to him.

A tear rolls down his cheek. "She was only twenty-three. Don't you feel anything for her?"

I shake my head no and say, "No, not a thing, but I do feel for you."

He reaches up and touches his chin.

"It's not too late for you," I tell him. "You can get out of this while you still have empathy."

"Get out of what exactly?" he asks with a quivering and

shaky voice, as if I am going to kill him or something.

"This line of work. It's changed you. You can still quit while you have feelings for people."

"Like you had for this person. He was twenty-five. He had just gotten out of college."

I look at the name. He shows me the picture. Then he shows me the shot to his face.

"Why? Why'd you shoot him in the face?"

This one had taken a long time. Three months, I stalked him, but he knew something was up. He watched his back. It was the first two that gave him a heads up. I wasn't very smart.

But every morning at five thirty, the paper boy would come. It was still dark. He was first on the route. I picked the paper up. The same as usual, he would come out, take his paper, go in, probably smoke a cigarette, drink a cup of coffee, and read his paper. Only he didn't smoke, and I had never seen him at a coffee shop.

But this day was different, as he looked for the paper.

"You looking for this?" I asked him.

"What?!?! You!!!" he said with a harsh angry voice.

I held the thick paper up in front of his face, and then I held up the .357 and shot it. When the bullet exited the chamber and hit the paper, it flattened that hollow point bullet out like a pancake. When it hit his face, it was like shrapnel going off from a hand grenade. The bullet went into his eye. There was hardly an eye socket there as it cleared its way through. What was left of his head bounced just a tad off the cement, and cold, without even calculating, I stood over him and shot him three times in the chest, right in the heart.

A year had gone by. I still hadn't shed a tear.

The sheriff settles down. His shaking somewhat goes away. "Well, Mr. Hourson, you gonna sign this?"

"It seems to be in order," I say.

No murder. Only killing.

My third confession.

"I'm a little hungry," I say.

"It's four in the morning. You're not gonna find much to eat for another four hours."

"Well, come back and see me then." I push all of it as far as I can with these chains on my wrists.

He picks up the unsigned paperwork and then the three signed papers, putting them on the bottom of the stack.

"A cup of coffee and a drink would be fine, too, with the meal," I add.

He pinches his lips together again. "I'll see what I can do."

While he is gone, I get to thinking about that fourth one.

She was thirty-nine. She had a family, but her kids were grown and gone. Her husband... It made me sick to think about it. I was at their back door. She was rich. It was a big place with a big stone wall that I laid up against as I listened carefully at the back door.

"You pick this up at the market, but make sure you're coming home when you do it. It has to go straight into the refrigerator. I like it fresh. You know that, right?" she says.

"Yes, dear. I'll take care of it."

Then I heard her loud footsteps going down the hallway, and I could hear him murmuring as he came to the back door, "As I do everything."

He opened the back door up to look down at me, but I wasn't there. "I can't do it at the house," I thought. "Her husband would get the blame, and that isn't what I want."

I got in my car and waited at the curb. It was down the road. It was a big ol' house. There were only three on the same side of the road. The blocks were kinda large, maybe a quarter mile before you got to the next turn. That's where I sat, in my car, and there she came, passing right by.

I was filled with disgust.

Rage, anger.

Then it went away, and I felt nothing.

It was a big building on campus. As usual, she worked. She clocked in. She went to work. She got off work. She went home.

I was almost transparent. I had learned to disguise myself many different ways. She had seen me three or four times, but she never knew it was me. And why would she? I looked in the mirror after disguising myself. It was too convincing. I didn't even know who I was myself.

At the back door again...

"I told you to pick this lettuce up after you got through with everything else. It's been out in the hot sun. It's all droopy. What good is that?"

"I did get it on the way home like you said."

"Then what's the matter with it? Why didn't you get a fresh head? Can't you do anything right?" She walked out of the room down the hall with her high heels again.

He came to the back door and threw the lettuce into the garbage. "This is the old head. The fresh head's in the refrigerator," he whispered lightly to himself. "If you would have just listened or opened up the fridge, you would have seen that. I was disposing of the old vegetables."

But it was that ugly little dog she had. It would snap at her husband and growl at him just as much as she did.

The sheriff comes in with the new paperwork and a lunch tray. "This is chopped steak, local diner. It's all they had."

It doesn't look that great, but I'm hungry. The taters are cold. I eat 'em anyway. The coffee is hot. After I take the last sip out of the drink and put the coffee cup and the drink on the tray, he pushes the fourth one to me.

"I talked to her husband," he says. "She wasn't a good person, it seems. Is that why you killed her?"

"A good person?" I say. "A bad person? They're all the same. You've been a cop in this town for years. Is there any innocent among you?" He doesn't say anything while I think there must not be since he doesn't answer.

12

But it was that dog. I had parked there many times, many days for many weeks. It was a long way down the road from her house when I saw that dog. Here she came, a long leash. I got out of the car and walked up to her to where she could see me.

"It's you!" she yelled out.

As soon as she spoke those words, she saw the gun. A frantic look came upon her face as the dog began to growl at me. Three times in the heart. The dog ran off, leash and all. So did I. Calm, cool, and collected.

———————

"That was the easiest one," I tell him.

"But why?"

"Like you said, she wasn't a good person."

He points at the line, for my signature, of course. "Mr. Hourson, you can sign now if you would like."

I ponder for a moment and look into his eyes. "You'll be thanking me before it's over."

He smiles real big. "Thanking you? They're gonna put you in the electric chair or death by lethal injection."

"It'll never happen, Sheriff."

He leans back quickly. "What?" he asks as fear comes upon his face again.

"You'll never charge me with it."

He pulls the piece of paper back, almost scared.

"Sheriff, I told you I would never hurt you. You have nothing to fear with me."

"Well, I thought you were fixing to break out or something. Are those handcuffs too tight around your wrists?"

I hold 'em up, both of 'em. "They're still there."

But he's shaken to the bone. I understand that. I have been there before.

It was eleven years ago, in my house. It was the thing I feared the most that happened. My wife had died years before that. It was just my daughter and I. She was a young teenager. I knew what fear was that night.

"Well, I'm gonna start processing these first four. You can read over the fifth one. I got all the paperwork changed over. No murder. As long as you confess that you killed 'em. No manslaughter. But that ain't no guarantee they won't charge you with it." After taking the tray, thinking on what I said, he disappears for quite a while.

Chapter 2
Killer

Killer.

They take me to my cell. I guess it's six hours later. I hear his voice in the background, talking to the other sheriffs.

"He ain't slept a bit, Sheriff," one of the deputies says. "He's just been sitting there, just like we left him."

Two deputies come and get me and take me back to the interrogation room. After they handcuff me and leave me there, here he comes with two cups of coffee.

"The D.A. wants you to confess to the murder and the killing. He feels like you're gonna try to get out of it the way you're doing it."

"Things are the way they are and the way they ought to be for a reason. When I'm through signing all these papers and you feel the need to change 'em and me resign 'em, then and only then will I do it," I tell him.

"Look, Mr. Hourson, apparently you feel you had a reason to kill these people, but look, this girl was twenty years old."

The fifth one.

The one I wanted dead the most.

I look at her picture. Her beautiful looks I despise. Her big blue eyes. They called her Sara.

"You made her suffer."

"Yes, I did."

"You shot her in the stomach and watched her until she almost died, and then you shot her in the heart." He slams his hand down. "Don't you know how much pain she was in?!?"

But yes...

———————

It was an apartment building. I got hired in as the janitor, a maintenance man, a clean up guy. I also got my room for free, my apartment. It was on the first floor. She was on the fifth. The top floor.

But I was looking down at her window, her bedroom window. It was the fire escape I was standing on. She never knew how long I stood there, staring at her, night after night. The flickering light from the building across the street. The last letter flickered, burning out or something. I don't know. I got a glimpse of her face every now and then.

I came down the stairway, and just like all the rooms of the building, keys.

———————

"Did I mention, Sheriff, how I love keys? I've got ten thousand keys, from all over the world, every kind of key you can imagine."

"Is that how you got into her apartment?"

I smile. "Of course. How else would you enter into a locked place?"

I pushed the key into the keyhole and turned it very slowly, along with the door knob. A bolt lock. "Now which one of these keys go to that? Oh, here it is." Five, ten.

There were ten apartments on each floor. Five on the left, and five on the right. The bedrooms stepped down a stairway onto the next floor, making each apartment a split level into the next apartment. Terrible design. When people were in the kitchen late at night, you could hear 'em through the bedroom wall.

It was my job to give each bedroom an extra lining of insulation to prevent the loud noises from coming through. It was the apartment beside her bedroom. It was empty. I had the wall down already, ready for the new insulation. It was great stuff. Three inches thick. It would reduce the sound by eighty percent.

The only thing that stood between her and I was a piece of thin sheet rock, and it was only three eighths of an inch thick. I punched a hole just big enough to see through. I observed her, staring at her for hours, thinking of how I hated her.

But I didn't really.

I didn't really feel anything for her.

I didn't feel anything at all.

I took the hole, put my finger in it, and pulled it toward me. After the hole got big enough, I stuck my whole arm in there and pulled a big chunk out. After making the hole big enough, I stepped into the room.

She woke up on the side of the bed as I stepped in. She pulled the covers up to her half clothed body. She was wide awake by then. I aimed the gun at her belly and pulled the trigger. I turned the lamp on as I pointed the gun up toward her head.

"Oh no, it's not you." She was panting for breath. "Oh God, it hurts so bad! Oh! Oh please don't kill me! Please!" she said as she held her hand up, as if I would stop.

"Okay."

"I've gotta get to a hospital. I'm dying," she said.

Her shortness of breath, it was getting worse. The pain was getting intolerable. She began to moan and groan. But the pain only got worse.

"I don't wanna die," she said with her crackling voice. Her prostonic look of dying. She laid back to her pillow. "I can't take it!" She cried the more. She tried to scream two or three times.

Her breathing eased up. She began to stare off and groan some more. "I can't take it!" she said.

She said it again, but I couldn't hear her. I got closer. "Please kill me," she whispered. "Please."

"I can't do that," I said. "You told me not to kill you."

"Please shoot me! Please!"

It was thirty long minutes. The groaning was with every breath she took. Until that point. Then, I could no longer hear her groan. She just whispered the same thing. "Kill me... kill me."

I aimed the gun at her chest and pulled the trigger three times. I cleaned up the sheet rock. I put a new wall up, painted it, went

18

back around, put the insulation up, and left no evidence that I was ever there.

"She suffered, you know."

"Yes, I know, Sheriff. I made sure of it."

He grabs the edge of the table with both hands and leans toward me. "Why? How could you be so cold?"

"You want me to sign?"

"At this point, I don't care if you sign or not." He wipes his hand across his mouth, and then he rubs his hand across the back of his neck as he stands up. He is trying to hide his emotions.

"Did you know her, Sheriff?"

"Everybody knew her. My daughter went to school with her."

"Did she like her?"

"I don't really know if she even knew her or not. I'm sure she might have."

He pushes the paperwork toward me. "Might as well get it over with."

I sign the paper.

It's Tuesday morning, going on about eleven o'clock. He walks out of the room. They put me back in my cell. After they feed me lunch, I guess it is about two o'clock when they put me back in the holding room to interrogate me some more.

It was the sixth one.

Slightly gray, suit and tie.

19

Executive type.

A business man, no doubt.

I knew who he was. I knew what he was.

He was a phony. The worst kind. They all were.

The first day, I followed him. He had a young family, a young wife. Twenty years younger than himself. He kissed his wife on the forehead and sat down to breakfast with his children. One was thirteen, and one was eight. I wasn't about to let them feel the pain that I felt. I wasn't gonna let them see the gruesonility of what was about to take place.

I had trouble with this one. I followed him for days. I almost didn't want to shoot him. But I know it was gonna happen. That I was sure of. He had to die.

It was a BMW. It was blue, a convertible. I had trouble keeping up. That thing would fly. From zero to ninety in nothing flat. My car was zero to one in an hour. I was doing sixty miles per hour when I came to a filling station and slid on the brakes. It was too late. I passed him.

This was my chance. I turned around, pulled in behind him, and got out. My bumper was two inches off of his bumper.

"Hey buddy, can you back it up a bit? I can't even walk between the cars," he said.

I had a hat on when I got out of the car. The rim was tilted down. He couldn't see my face.

"Hey, did you hear me? Move your damn car."

I looked up as I pulled the cannon out. "You??!? How is that even possible?" he tried to exclaim.

But before he could get the word possible out, I had already shot him in the heart three times. I tilted my hat back down, got in my car, and left. I backed out and back down the road. The owner got my tags. I then went to a junkyard and had the car destroyed. I knew that would happen. I had bought it for that reason, and as far as the tags went, I had stolen 'em off his other car.

"He had a family, you know," the sheriff says.

"I know."

"He was good to 'em."

"As far as they know, he was."

"You care to elaborate?" the sheriff asks.

"Sure, but I thought you wanted me to sign this paper."

"How do you do it?"

"How do I do what?"

"You're so cold. Uncalculating. No emotion at all. You scare me."

"That's not my intent. There's good reason."

"There's never a good reason to murder, to kill people."

"Really Sheriff? How many times have you pulled the trigger?"

He hangs his head in shame quickly. It is his response that changes things. "More than I should have. It could have been less."

"You made the decision though. Didn't you? Judge. Executioner."

"Mr. Hourson, it's totally different. You murdered these

people."

"I've never murdered anybody in my life," I say very angrily and very quickly.

He wipes his mouth again. He is troubled really bad. He stands up and wipes the back of his neck again. He shakes his head.

"What's the matter, Sheriff?"

"Just sign the paper," he says.

I put my signature on the paper.

"Mr. Hourson, I just don't understand how you can be so cold about all this. You seem like an alright guy. It don't even seem possible that you could be the one to do this."

"Sheriff, I did it. I shot 'em. Just like I said I did."

"Mr. Hourson! This is cold blooded murder! In the first degree!"

I ball my fists up. "It's not murder!"

That's when he throws the pictures on the table. "How do you explain all this?!?" He shakes his hands. He's terribly troubled.

"You want me to sign the papers, Sheriff, I'll sign 'em. Every one of 'em."

He pushes the other six in front of me. "Then sign away," he says with an angry voice.

I ponder on the next one. Twenty-eight, fresh out of college. But you would have hardly known it. He was raring to go, fresh. He was new in the company that he started working for and was only too eager to move up. More eager than I was willing to deal with.

I stare at his picture.

No feeling whatsoever.

I don't hate. I don't love.

I just don't feel anything.

"I'm hungry, Sheriff. Why don't you go fetch me something to eat?"

"Fetch you something? I thought we were in the respectable mode."

"Yeah, but that ended long ago. I've been six hours without eating, using the bathroom, or anything to drink. And every hour, you walk out that door. You either get you something to drink, smoke a cigarette—"

"I don't smoke," he says.

"I don't care," I tell him. "By Friday, you'll be shaking my hand, thanking me."

He puts his palms down on the table and looks at me cold in the eyes. "There's no way in hell that I'm *ever* gonna shake your hand."

"I'll hold you to that, Sheriff. Now go fetch me something to eat."

"Alright, mister! I'll get you something to eat," he growls.

When he comes back this time, he comes back with a little respect. It's a hot meal, and it's fresh. A cold drink. I eat it right down as if it's my last meal. I don't leave anything on the plate.

"Hungry were you? That ain't a famine. That's starvation. You like your steak?"

"It's pretty decent. I like a little red coming out of it. Just a little bit."

He swallows deep. I can tell I turned his stomach when I said that with all those pictures on the table. The fact is, I like my steak well done. I don't like any red at all, but I don't tell him that. I'm upset with him.

"Mr. Hourson, can we get on with the program?"

Tuesday afternoon. The day is far spent when a detective walks in and hands the sheriff a report. The sheriff gets up and walks out of the room for a moment. I have now been in this room for twenty-four hours, not including the time I sat over in the cell. My back is hurting. My bottom is numb, and I am chained to a chair. I stand up for a moment, but unable to leave the chair, I don't stay on my feet very long.

Here comes a deputy. "Alright, you, come on. Don't try anything funny. There's two more deputies outside the door."

"Don't worry. I ain't going nowhere."

He looks at me. "I ain't too sure about that. They put killers to death in this state."

"No, they don't."

"Yes, they do, Mister."

"They put murderers to death in this state. Not killers."

"Well, that's sure enough what you are is a killer. Now come on, killer."

"Okay, I deserve that."

"You might as well get used to it. Everybody's calling you that. You're the talk of the show now. Now you get on in that cell, and you... you..."

"What's the matter, Deputy? I make you nervous?"

"Well, you'd make any normal person nervous."

"Got some guilt riding on you there, Deputy?"

"Nothing like you should have. All those people you murdered."

I give him an angry look and say, "I never murdered anybody."

"Look, mister. I done seen the paperwork. You signed it."

"What's the matter, Deputy? You ain't never killed nobody before?"

"I ain't never killed nobody that didn't deserve it. Besides that, I only killed one person." He looks to see if anybody is looking, and then he says, "And I ain't too sure it wasn't by accident, but it was in self defense."

"So you accidentally defended yourself." I say it out loud.

"Hush up, now! You hear!"

"It's okay, Deputy. Your secret's safe with me."

"It ain't no secret. I been doing desk work ever since then. But you oughta be ashamed of yourself. You just a killer."

"Fair enough. We're both killers, but I'm a cold blooded killer."

"I'm a Deputy Sheriff. I killed a man in the line of duty. Where's your honor?"

"My honor? I'll tell you where my honor is..."

Chapter 3
Momma's Son

It isn't 'til the next day. Back to the holding room. Interrogation starts all over. This time, a detective walks in. "Do you know me?" he asks.

"No, I don't know you." But I know his kind.

"I'll be taking over the case," he says.

"What's the matter? The sheriff couldn't handle it?"

"Well, it's not really his department, but he had been doing the investigation on this for quite a while. But it was something you said that got to him. You won't get to me so easily."

"Ah, you been around a little?" I ask him.

"I've been around a lot," he answers, which only could mean that he's killed a lot of people, which leaves his innocence questionable.

"How did you get those scars on your face?" he asks me.

"Does it matter?"

"Says here in your report that your wife died. What? Thirteen years ago?"

"Fourteen."

"You had a kid. Laurie? Is that her name?"

"That's her name."

"The deputy said when he brought you in here out of your cell that you haven't been sleeping. Said you sat up all night."

"It's nothing new, Detective. I sit up all night every night. I haven't slept for ten long years."

"There's some pages missing out of this report. You know how that came about?"

"Ah, it'll show up, I'm sure. Then you'll know everything."

"Oh, we know everything already. You were caught red handed. And that gun, it was in your name. It was like you bought it for this purpose."

But it was only too true. I had bought it just to kill.

"So how did you lose it?"

"I didn't."

"Come on, now. It fall out of your pants when you sat down? Or did you lay it down and just forget it? Nah, you don't look like the type."

I just sit there.

"Mr. Hourson. That's a fine Christian name you got there, Mr. Hourson."

"Yes, it is," I say. "Along with my family."

"You don't seem the church type to me."

"That's 'cause I don't go to church."

"No, but you used to."

I look up at him, wondering how he knows.

"Where's your daughter at?"

"It's all in the report."

"Well, fill me in. That part of the report's gone."

But I don't say anything.

"Six of these are unsigned," he says as he goes through the folders. "So you don't think you're a murderer, but you are a killer."

"Oh, I'm a killer, alright. That's what I confessed to is killing. Only killing. Never murdered. No manslaughter involved."

That's when his pager goes off. "Dang! I'll have to get back with you on this." He is called off to another scene.

But the detective, he was angry from the time he walked in the door and even more angry when he saw me, but I could tell he was trying to blow it off. I could also tell he wasn't a good person.

Maybe it was while he was on duty. Having to kill somebody. Nah, it couldn't be that. It happens way too often.

This one's had three partners disappear. When the ambulance carried 'em off to the morgue. He called 'em all three in. "My partner's down. The assailant got away." But three times, and still made detective. He's got an angel watching over him.

But it was the sweating that he did. He wasn't even there five minutes, and all he could talk about was himself. I this, I that. It was more the expressions than it was the words. With only a few words and over a thousand expressions, now this one was trouble.

But it's that silly deputy that comes and gets me. "You done got everybody worked up around here. There's people out there with signs that don't like you."

"You better read the signs again, Deputy."

But I haven't been outside. Neither have I seen any news.

"Oh, I read the sign alright. I can spell killer."

"I didn't mean no offense, Deputy, but everybody knows I'm a killer. That has been well established. But the question is, where do we go from here?"

"Well, I'll tell you where you're going. You're going back to your cell."

Chapter 4
Nina

Wednesday morning. I could smell it before it even came. Coffee. Here comes the sheriff back, along with two deputies. Back to the interrogation room.

"Can we just get this over with?" He puts the folders out there and takes the first sheet out of each one of 'em.

"I thought you gave up on me, Sheriff."

"Well, I didn't wanna miss the chance to shake your hand Friday. Besides, the detective was...uh...well, somebody pulled him off the case. Some judge. He looked pretty upset about it."

"So he gets the most important parts. Is that what you're saying?"

"Important parts?"

Yeah, when the shooting goes on, he's there. When the paperwork goes on, you're there," I answer.

"Now look, Mr. Hourson, I thought we were on the respectable side again."

"Yeah, why don't you keep it there?"

"Alright, mister, from right now 'til Friday, you're gonna get my respect. I'm gonna give you the benefit of the doubt. Even though I'm deeply troubled about this whole ordeal. A killer who's convinced he's not a murderer, and everyone here believes it's a murderer convinced that he's just a crazy killer."

"And you?"

"Killing, murdering, it's all the same. You killed people, and you're gonna get the chair for it."

"Sheriff, they don't do the chair in this state. It's lethal injection."

"You know what I mean."

"I know what you mean alright."

"The seventh one. Twenty-eight years old."

"You know the story, Sheriff, but I'm gonna tell you a little bit about this one. How I did it, and how I felt while I was doing it. Yeah, I shot him in the chest, and you wanna know how I felt?"

"I'm listening," the Sheriff says.

"I felt relieved. I felt like a hero."

I sign my name to the seventh one, but it's the eighth one that's gonna move him.

Another young lady in her twenties. They called her Nina, but that was just her nickname, at least that's all that I really knew. She liked to encourage people to do things, but she would have to suffer. I didn't like her. Right from the start. She was not a good person.

Sexually overactive.

31

A Barbie doll.

Rich, arrogant, flaunty.

That was her attitude.

But only her best friends knew who she really was. To everyone else, she turned from coal to diamonds.

The world belongs to me type.

A world that I would take away.

I stepped into her rich little apartment. Four thousand a month. She didn't work. She didn't have to. Daddy had been long gone, only to leave his money behind.

I ask the sheriff, "Why is it somebody could have so much to do so much good with and do nothing at all with it?"

Waste.

I hate waste.

"She was found dead in the shower," the sheriff says. "She suffered, too."

"I made sure of it," I say to him. "She liked to do things without her clothes. I thought she oughta die without 'em. She liked to impregnate pain but never on herself."

"So you shot her in the stomach?"

"Yes, I shot her in the stomach but not with a hollow point. It was a full metal jacket. It went straight through, right into the shower wall. She sank down. I shot right through the glass. I didn't even get to see her until the glass fell out of the door. Some of it fell on her leg. That's what cut her."

"So you didn't cut her leg?"

32

"No, I didn't put the cuts on her."

"Well, that added to her pain, along with the shot in the belly that you gave her. How long did it take her?"

"Forty-five minutes."

"You stood there forty-five minutes?!?! The two prettiest. The most beautiful girls I've ever seen. And you made 'em suffer an unbelievably painful death!"

"Yes, I did. Both of 'em."

"You say it as if they deserved it."

"Deserve? We all deserve death. Every one of us," I say as I look him dead in the eye.

"Mr. Hourson, I feel like there's a lot you're not telling me."

"Well, I'm sorry you feel that way, Sheriff. I'll tell you whatever you want me to tell you, whatever you want to know."

"Well, I just wanna make sense of all this."

But I understand that only too well.

Senseless killings.

And for what?

"And they're so random," he says.

"Random? These are not random. They were not chosen out of a crowd. They were the crowd. Innocent? The innocent are dead and gone."

"Well, she sure looked innocent to me."

"So do prostitutes lying on a autopsy table. So does a priest when cancer has eaten his lungs, his liver, and his throat to where he can't talk anymore. So did my wife, who died from cancer in severe pain after serving God her whole life."

"You're mad at God? Is that why you're killing everybody?"

"Mad at God? I thanked God."

"Oh, so now you're a religious man?"

"Religious? Not at all. I'm nowhere close to religious."

He lets out a breath. "Humph. I would call for the psychiatrist, but I don't believe you're crazy."

"I'm not crazy, Sheriff. I'm not insane. I'm not crazy. I'm just exactly what you said."

"Killer?"

"If that's what you want to call me. I did kill people. But murder, no. I'm not a murderer."

"Okay, killer."

"Really Sheriff?"

"Seems like that's what you were trying to do, build up your name, so I might as well start calling you killer."

I look at him. "So is that what I call you?"

He smiles and says, "Okay, that's not fair. You're wanting the reputation of a killer."

"No, I'm not, Sheriff. The fact is I wouldn't hurt a fly."

He smiles real big, and he slams his hand down on the table again. "Those girls didn't stand a chance, and you talk about having compassion for a fly. You watched 'em bleed out. Crying. In pain. And right before their hearts stopped beating, you put three bullets in 'em, blowing their hearts out their backs."

"Just fulfilling the promise."

"Oh, now we're going to the Bible, are we?"

I laugh. "The Bible? Is that what you think this is about? Some religious fanatic. Another religious fanatic gone crazy. Mad at God. That's not what this is about. If anything, I did God a

34

favor."

"Mr. Hourson, these were not prostitutes, pimps, murderers."

"Worse!" I say.

"These were people of society, doing what they thought was right."

"Really? I'm people of society, too, and I did what I know what was right."

"If I let you go right now— I'm not going to by the way— but if I let you go right now, tell me the truth, would the killing stop?"

"The killing stopped when you found my gun. That wasn't a stroke of work that your deputies put out. Long, hard investigative work. They couldn't find their way out of a closet. I laid that gun down there for you to find it, Sheriff."

"You must have thought it was gonna make you a hero when we found you."

"Yeah, I kinda thought that. But then I put pride and arrogance in front of that, and here we are."

"You know, I hope they stick it to you. I hope they put that stuff in your veins."

"No, you don't."

He rubs his mouth again. He pushes the other paper toward me. "Didn't you feel anything? She was twenty something years old. She wasn't even out of college yet."

"You know that college ain't all it's cracked up to be, Sheriff."

"You know something about the college?"

Then wheels start spinning in his head. He starts connecting people. They were all affiliated with the college. We have a good conversation. It lasts for hours, but he only ends it thinking my imagination is extremely vivid and wonders if he can believe anything I say. But up 'til now, he has no reason not to.

"Mr. Hourson, you're not telling me something, and it's vital importance needs to be rectified. Just why did you kill these people?"

I lean back in my chair as I sign the eighth one and push it back toward him. "Yeah, now that's the question I've been waiting to hear."

"I've already asked you."

"Yeah, but without all that arrogance. By Friday, you're gonna be a hero. You're gonna shake my hand and thank me."

He leans back toward his seat. He knows I believe what I'm saying. "I don't see how that is even possible. You've killed twelve people in cold blood, murdered them in plain view for people to see. There's witnesses. You confessed. And yet you still think I'm gonna shake your hand and thank you for it."

But as I had spoken, things had come together in his head. It was the long hours that I hinted around.

A secret.

An untold secret.

A secret so devastating that not anyone should know the truth.

The sheriff, I don't think he really wanted to know the truth.

But it had to be told.

The secret had to be revealed.

Just to him.

But before it revealed itself, I had to play along.

"Maybe you oughta call that doctor in you were talking about if you think I'm crazy," I say.

"No, you're not crazy, but if this happens, I'll not only shake your hand, but I'll take you out to the finest restaurant in this city."

"Well, I'll be looking forward to that, Sheriff. I also want your resignation."

"Yeah? Why is that, Mr. Hourson?"

"Because you need to get out of this before it steals what little empathy you've got left for people."

He rubs his hand on his face again, right across his mouth, and back through his neck, he rubs again He ponders for a moment and then opens the next folder.

She was an elderly woman, always doing something for the community. Walk-a-thons, hot dog fundraisers, things to raise money for the city orphans. I hated her the most. Once a month, she would go to a meeting.

A late night meeting.

The unwedded truth about who she really was.

I knew.

Do gooders. They always try to do good because in their heart, they've done so much wrong. Mere penance isn't good enough. They've gotta right their wrong. If that was the case at all.

But in her case was me.

The adjuster.

The adjuster of truth between what would and would not be.

Between life and living.

These people were not living.

I knocked on her door in broad daylight. "Well, hello, young man. Oh my God! It's you! How did you—"

Three times, quick and clean, right in the heart. She was gurgling up blood, still trying to say, "How did you? How?" And then she died.

"It was quick, but she was an old woman."

"You had compassion on her, didn't you? Not cold and calculating like the last two. The two blondes with blue eyes. The little girls you killed. I've got the feeling that you hate blonde haired, blue eyed girls, especially pretty ones."

But on the contrary. I was in love with the most beautiful one of all. Where was her justification? Where were those that had empathy and kindness for her? Where was the drive to save her life?

"It's just like the boys at the orphanage and the girls there," I tell him and wait a moment to let him think on that. "How come you never get a report that they're missing or gone?"

"Mr. Hourson, kids run away from that orphanage every week."

"Do they? All at the age of ten years old, eleven years old, virgins. Really? They just get up and run away, do they? You ever heard from any of them again?"

"Just exactly what are you getting at, Mister?"

"Don't lose the respect, Sheriff. Come next Monday, I'll be

the most respected person in your life."

He grins real big. "More metaphors."

"It's getting late, Sheriff. You better go have lunch with your wife or dinner or supper, whatever you call the seven o'clock meal."

He looks down at his watch. His eyes get big. He starts gathering up his paperwork as if he is late for something. He goes out the door.

"Get him back in his cell. Get him what he wants," he tells the deputies.

The deputies come in. "Looks like you won some favor with the sheriff. He said, get the man what he wants. What do you think about that, killer?"

I smile and say, "You'll be the new sheriff coming next week."

He looks down at his hands. "Man, do you see the color of my hands?"

I say, "Man, you'll be the new sheriff next week."

He smiles real big and says, "You know, killer? I kinda like you."

As he takes me back to my cell, holding his hand on my back in the center of it and holding my arm gently leading the way, he says, "Matter of fact, I like you so much, I'm gonna come and visit your grave 'cause I know they gonna kill you."

I smile at him as I hear the door clink behind me.

"You know you could rest a lot easier if you could just forgive yourself," he says.

I smile at him again. "Deputy, I forgave myself ten years ago when I was unable to save my daughter."

"Well, I'm sorry about your daughter. I didn't know you had a daughter," the deputy says. "We've got a report on you, but it don't say nothing about your daughter."

"I know." I smile when I say that.

He looks at me and says, "You know, I ain't very smart, but I get the feeling you're playing us. I guess I'll just wait and see."

I sit there on the bed, all night again.

Chapter 5
Dirty Deeds

There that smell is. Coffee. The deputy comes early, before the sheriff comes. "I told you I was beginning to like you. Look there, I done brung you a cup of coffee."

"Thanks, Deputy."

"How come you don't act like a killer? Oh yeah, when you first came in, you had us all scared and stuff."

"And now?"

"Well, I don't know. But I get the feeling I'm better off with you sometimes than I am with some of these deputies."

"Like the detective?"

His eyes get real big. He looks around. "What'd you say?"

"You heard me."

He says, "I better not bring you no more coffee. It's gone to your head."

"But I haven't drank any coffee yet."

"Well, I'll just take this back."

"Now don't be like that, Deputy."

"Okay, I'll leave the coffee, but no more talking like that. You hear?"

"Yeahhhhh."

"Sometimes I feel like I oughta be working for you," he mutters as he walks out the door.

I sip on the coffee as I say, "But you are, working on my good side."

Tomorrow will be Friday. Here comes the sheriff. "You got a couple of more pages to go. You sure you wanna go through with this, being that I'm gonna be shaking your hand tomorrow afternoon?"

"I didn't say tomorrow afternoon, Sheriff."

"No, but you did say tomorrow."

He looks at me real sovereign like. "I kinda wish it would be like you said, me shaking your hand and all, but I just don't see how that's possible, Mr. Hourson."

He opens the door by himself this time. I say, "Sheriff, you're taking a big chance, ain't you?"

"Yeah, I am, but with good reason. Now come on, let's go to the interrogation room."

I walk around the door. I walk out of the cell. I walk down the hall. I walk straight into the interrogation room, slide the bracelet back on my wrist, and slide down into the chair, waiting for him to put the other one on.

He doesn't.

He sits down, pushes his hands up through the front part of his hair, and halfway through, he begins to scratch. Then he begins to scratch really hard on the side of his head, then puts his hands on his lap, and then blows out some breath.

Now this one is what is shaking the whole police department because I failed to say that the other one I shot, the blonde that I made suffer, the one they called Sara, her dad was a policeman. I shot him in the belly, also, at his house.

As I stood over him, he said, "You can't shoot me. You can't kill me this way. I'm a cop."

"You ain't no cop. No real cop would let me get the drop on him like this."

"We should've made sure we finished the job," he said. His eyes iced over, cold, the way I stood there, wishing that he would have lived a little longer and suffered a little more.

I shot him in the heart. "That's for her."

I shot him again. "That's for everyone else you killed that I cared so much about."

I shot him the third time. The bullet must have hit the backbone and ricocheted off the floor back into his neck bone because his whole body flopped up into a sitting position, real fast, and then slowly fell back to the floor.

My eyes got big. "That's for me, and for not finishing the job."

When you run up against a killer, that's a fatal mistake.

That was three years ago. They found the guy that did it, executed him without a trial, and now I'm confessing to his death.

It was only after they killed him when they found out the truth, that he wasn't the killer.

"Yeah, I killed him. Just like I did the others. He didn't suffer like his daughter did, but I tried."

"Did you know he was a dirty cop?"

"All the cops in this town are dirty," I say. "It just ain't 'til they're on the take that they realize it."

I tilt my head a little bit and open my eyes as I raise my eyebrows and look at him. He looks at my eyes at first, then he looks at my mouth. He doesn't know what to say.

Another executive. Some type of city official. He was the one with the medallion around his neck. Some kind of high priest, he tried to act like, I guess, but you could you tell he was more like a joke. But it was no joke to me.

Another do gooder.

A hand shaker.

If you were facing him, you were guaranteed to see a smile, but it was when people walked away... If nobody was looking, he was never smiling.

Gray suit.

The smell of tobacco.

Pipe tobacco.

But he remembered me. "It can't be you! How's that even possible?" he said.

It was the lobby of a darkened hotel, old in its age. He was the owner, no doubt, along with other buildings and other miscellaneous things. I thought about how to make him suffer, but when he reached to grab me with his hands, I shot off his knee. He flopped on the floor until he had a heart attack.

Foam began to come up out of his mouth, but he began to mumble words, "I...i...i... it wasn't my idea. It... wasn't... my... idea." And then he died.

"No, it might not have been your idea, but..."

"What wasn't his idea, Mr. Hourson?"

"I guess you'll have to ask him that, Sheriff."

Thursday afternoon. The sheriff feeds me good. That's when they get a call. Another homicide. The detective lost another partner. The assailants got away. They left the gun. I spend another night in the cell.

Chapter 6
Not My Daughter

Friday morning. Here comes the sheriff.

I say, "Sheriff, how come it is somebody shoots a cop and leaves the gun at the scene of the crime? And how come it is that the gun's got no serial number and it's taped up to where no fingerprints could get on it? No DNA?"

The sheriff looks at me. He has been pondering on it already.

"It only took all week, and we ain't got but two signatures to go. Let's make haste, shall we?"

He pulls out the eleventh one.

———————————

Thirty-three years old. She was breathtaking. She made friends with everybody. Never said anything wrong. She walked everywhere she went. She refused to drive. She dated a few guys, but when they refused to give up their cars, she called 'em polluters.

"I'm an environmentalist, and I love my environment." She

had logos everywhere. Everybody knew her in the city. She was way too popular.

I didn't make her suffer. She woke up out of a dead sleep. "Who is it? I know you're there."

It was a very comfortable chair. It was plush lined and very smooth to the skin. Very elegant. I sat there very quietly. I pulled the hammer back. She turned the light on. She was scared for her life until she saw my face, and then a sovereign look came upon her face.

"I watched you die," she said.

Three times in the heart. "And I watched you die," I said.

"So you mean to tell me you had mercy on this one?"

"Yeah, Sheriff. See, the fact is, I was in love with her. We were gonna get married."

"This was your fiance'?!?!"

"I didn't say that. I never actually proposed. She had other intentions in spite of my mood."

"Your mood?"

"I don't think she would have went through with it."

"Mr. Hourson, went through with what? What are you talking about?"

I pick up the pen and sign my name as I have done with the others. "One more to go."

He takes his elbow off of his knee, leans back a little bit, and puts both of his hands on his knees. But things are starting to turn in his head, and just as I suspected, he is beginning to see things.

"Sheriff? You carry a revolver, don't you?"

"That's right. What about it?"

"How come it is that you ain't never loaded it, and you don't let nobody know about it? You ain't never told nobody that but one person, and he's running the whole show."

"Mr. Hourson, this ain't no circus, and this ain't no show. And how did you know that? You been talking to the detective. He's the only one that knew that. If you've got something to say, say it."

"I've been saying it all along. You just haven't been listening. You need to load that gun. Put your bullets back in the cylinders."

"We still gonna come out shaking hands?"

I smile. "I sure hope it turns out that way, Sheriff, because if it doesn't, that means one of us will be dead."

His eyes get big. "I thought you wouldn't ever hurt me."

"Hurt you? I'm gonna try to save you if I can."

"Okay, that's... Now it's gone far enough. I tell you what, sign this last one, and I'm gonna put you back in your cell."

"Sheriff, why do you keep looking at the door? You expecting somebody? It's a hard thing to know something's going on that you can't stop, but yet you can't do nothing about it when you're dead in the middle of it."

His eyes get even bigger. He holds his lips together, pulls out his revolver, opens the cylinder, and puts five big bullets in it. "Okay, you got my attention," he says. "When's all this gonna happen?"

"Right after I sign this last one and you take me back to my cell."

He closes the cylinder, puts the gun back in the holster, shakes his head backward and forward, and says, "I sure hope you're wrong, but I got a scary feeling..."

She was fifty-nine. She had gotten married again after her husband died. When the sheriff pulls out the name and the picture, after so many times that he has done it before, this time, he sees her eyes.

"I've seen those eyes before," he says.

I smile a little bit and sit back while the wheels turn.

It was just three months ago. "I love you, too, son. We'll see you at the next gathering, huh? What's this, our fourth one this year?"

"Just two more, and we'll have all the power we need."

"Okay, I love you. Goodbye."

I pulled the hammer back. "Oh, I knew it was you. You've killed my whole clan, but you won't get my so..."

I shot her in the heart before she could finish what she was saying. She was still alive. "It's too late," she said. "There's a new order. He will be running the whole—"

Then, she died, after I put two more holes in her heart.

Now I had a little habit about my gun. I had three hollow points and three full metal jackets. Sometimes I would separate 'em, one after another one, a hollow point, then a full metal jacket, and sometimes I wouldn't. It would be three on one side and three on the other one. It depended on how much I wanted 'em to suffer and how fast I wanted 'em to die. The full metal jacket would make 'em suffer more, but the hollow points were quick and painless. I was a killer.

I take the pen out of my mouth, click the ball point outward, and begin to sign my name.

"Deputies, get in here! Get this man in restraints. Get him back to his cell."

He looks down the hall and then opens the door. When we get down to the cell door, he opens the outer door, and then he opens the cell door and takes my restraints off.

"You good, Sheriff?" one deputy asks.

"Yeah, you good, Sheriff?" the other asks.

"Yeah, I got it from here," he says.

I walk farther into my cell and turn around.

"Boy, you had us all going there for a while."

"Did I, Sheriff?"

"I believed everything you said there for the last two days."

"And now?"

He scratches the side of his head and walks on the other side of the door. But that's when he turns around and sees the door opening slowly. I stand back, and he steps back a little bit, too. Behind the door. The door finishes opening.

He steps in, pulling an old looking shotgun out. It's a pump police special. He lowers it down slowly.

The sheriff cries out, "Detective! What are you doing?!?!"

He points the gun at him, but before he can get it fully appointed, the sheriff shoots him right in the head.

The deputy comes in, the one that kinda likes me "Sheriff! What have you done?!?!"

"He was gonna murder him. He tried to kill me. He tried to shoot me first."

That's when he rolls him off of his shotgun. It isn't even part of the police station. It has the serial numbers scratched off.

"Okay, Mr. Hourson, it's time to tell me what's going on."

I say, "The last one I shot was his mother. It happened eleven years ago. You know the cop I shot? His daughter befriended my daughter. They went to the mall. They became a part of my family. The young guys, she met up with them at the mall, and my twelve year old daughter went with her and then to the movies. I put a stop to it after I found out the guys were going, especially that younger one. I could tell he didn't really want to go through with it."

I have been telling the sheriff this story all week long.

"Go through with what?" the sheriff asks.

"I'm trying to tell you, Sheriff."

Day after day, week after week, they got closer. The woman I was in love with and all the rest of 'em, they played us good, my daughter and I, making us think that they were family and that they loved us. They seemed so wonderful.

One night, one had my wrist. One had my ankle. One had my other ankle. One had my head. One had my other wrist, and two of them had my waist as they carried me out the door vertically. They found use for tie wraps as they strapped me to the inner liner of the van. I gave one good pull, and the liner cut right through the band. That's when they put my hands behind my back in handcuffs, police handcuffs, and tried it again.

"That really hurts. What are you guys doing? Why are you doing this? We're friends. We're family almost."

But it was the cop. "Tonight's initiation night for my daughter. Hemlin and the rest are waiting for you."

It was in the city beneath a building, deep in the cellar of it. The ceiling must have been forty feet high. There was a solid block column in the middle. The woman I was in love with was there, along with the rest of the twelve. They all wore black clothes with black hoods.

I was scared to death. I shook, but when I saw them bring my daughter in and strap her to that block, I was horrified. She had no clothes on. My wrists were bleeding from trying to get away. My ankles were broken. No matter much I stressed to get away, it just made matters worse.

The cop's daughter, the second blonde I killed, Sara, Hemlin put the dagger in her hand. "Commence the initiation."

She walked up to my daughter. Nina, the other blonde was routing her on. "Don't be a wimp," she said. "I've already had my initiation. I already feel the power. There's nothing like it."

I was gagged. I cried while I tried to speak. She said, "I can't do it. I'm not going to do it."

Her dad walked up. "Do it for the family," he said.

I didn't know what he meant until just now. Once in, no out. When you get out, your family who ain't even in there gets out, too. The only way out is death.

She shook her head yes and got up on my daughter as the other blonde routed her on. She slowly pushed the dagger into my

52

daughter's chest while she screamed so hard and so loud that she turned purple. Then, she finished pushing the dagger on in. But she didn't feel the power. She felt the curse of death. It swallowed her up.

Things got dark after that. I passed out. My daughter disappeared, along with me. They threw me in a ravine after stabbing me. I floated down. How I even lived is a miracle. I ended up on a sandbar, and this old woman in this jalopy of a motor boat picked me up. There was only enough room for me to lay down with my feet hanging overboard and her to sit on the back. She took me to this little cabin.

I woke up on a bed. "If you live, you're gonna owe me. If you die, I'm gonna feed you to my alligators. Deal?"

I cried bitterly.

"Deal?" she said again.

I shook my head yes as I went ahead and let it go.

"Been through a tough one, have you? Well, I got news for you, honey. We've all been through it. One time or another one. I could tell you a story or two if you wanna hear it."

But I didn't. I turned my head. She set my feet. My ankles were crooked.

"Looks like you had a run-in with the mob. Had my time with them a time or two. Time'll heal it. Time'll heal it all. I got even with 'em though," she said. "Took me twenty-five years."

She began to tell the story of how she had knocked 'em off one by one. How she set 'em up to fall from within. She put ideas in my head. Disgusting ideas.

I repaid the old woman not too long before she died. She told me how they had put her in prison, but when I told her my story, she wiped the tears out of her eyes as she got up out of her old rocking chair.

"That beats anything I ever been through. Yep," she stopped in the middle of the floor after walking across. "That beats anything I ever been through," she repeated and walked on out.

It was six weeks before I could walk. It was almost a year before I said a word. The last thing I asked her as I stood over her dead body, his mother, the detective's mother: "Where's my daughter? What did y'all do with my daughter's body?"

But she didn't say anything.

The sheriff looks at me. "Mr. Hourson, we found your daughter. We labeled her as Jane Doe. But that was over ten years ago. She was among the first that disappeared. We had no idea who she was. Her fingerprints were gone, and her blood was drained. Without family there, we had no way of identifying her."

But now the sheriff has no more questions to ask. He opens the door to my cell. "I understand it all now."

Chapter 7
Death's At The Door

It has been a twelve year investigation. They call themselves the Elite Empowerment, the t double e. They had sacrificed the children, each one a sacrifice. Every one had to prove that they weren't afraid to take a life. But it wasn't just any life. They had to be pure, frigid in every way, and they had to be their best friends, the best of friends. The power to take a life. It's easy to take an enemy's life or someone you don't know, but someone you care for and love, they were perfect victims.

The sheriff shows me the trail he has been on, but there is still another. There always is. I spend another six hours in detail. I have just about wrapped it up. But there is one thing we failed to include, and it isn't going to go undone.

The orphanage.

After intimate details, it is seven o'clock Friday afternoon. "Well, I guess this is where we part ways."

I smile real big and put out my hand. He looks down and smiles real big, also. And then he shakes my hand. "Thanks."

"For what, Sheriff?"

"After today, I won't be sheriff any more," he says. "The old deputy's gonna be the new sheriff."

"Good luck with that," I tell him.

"Oh yeah, Sheriff," I say before he leaves, "you still owe me a five star restaurant dinner, but I'm gonna let you slide this time," I say.

He says, "How about Burger King instead?"

"I'm gonna take a rain check on that."

I leave the sheriff's station, but I am more than a little disturbed. It is late Friday night. I have intentions of breaking into the police station. Evidence room. I am going to have to get past a guard after picking a lock, get in, get what I want, get out, and all without being seen.

One o'clock in the morning. The guard on duty gets to relieve himself every hour for fifteen minutes when another one takes his place. Only this time, it is ten minutes too early when he has to go to the restroom. There is a wedge that holds the door open when they bring evidence in. Well, he just sticks that wedge on in and goes on to the bathroom. "Nothing ever happens here anyway," he thinks.

I walk right on in. It's the medallion and the cape with the hood. I walk out just as I walked in. Unheard and unseen.

Three o'clock in the morning. A knock on the door. A horrid looking woman comes to the door. I have the hood over my face, the medallion hanging around my neck.

"You were supposed to have been here yesterday, and a lot earlier. I've only got one this time. The sheriff and his deputies came asking questions. This one won't be missed. Don't you worry about that."

"Two," I say to the woman, so she will obviously go to somebody in charge.

I follow her closely. "You can't come in here. You know the rules."

I hold up my fingers and say two.

She walks into an office. "They can't settle for one tonight. They need two."

I get closer 'til I can see who it is. I push my hand on the door. "Where's your ring?" she asks. "You're not the head master."

But the one thing I have forgotten. I don't have my gun anymore. I have no money to buy one either. I have lived in a hut for the past... Well, for a long time. I had a good job, made a lot of money for a little while. Obsession.

I was beside myself for years. I could still hear her voice. "Daddy, please help me!" But I couldn't say anything. Yes, I was beside myself.

The old woman died crying over... Well, she said my story was the saddest she had ever heard.

This one is ready for me. He shoots the woman twice, trying to shoot me. I get down the hallway. He comes out of the door before I get to the end, so I jump into a doorway that is barely cracked open. There is no light. A flight of rugged wooden steps. Oh, it busts me good, two or three times. My elbow, my knee, and my shin. It gives me a good gash. It hurts so bad!

As soon as I get to feeling it real good, three shots are fired right beside me, and then the light turns on. Before his eyes get adjusted, I jump out of the way just in time for him to shoot right where I had been.

He carefully walks down the steps, bending over, watching every move, if there would have been a move. And there isn't. Everything is quiet. The first squeaky step he steps on is like something out of a horror flick. When he steps down to the third step, a hand reaches up and grabs his ankle. As he steps down with the other foot, another hand grabs the other ankle.

They are my hands. I walk over to where he landed. He points that gun up to my head and pulls the trigger.

"You've done had your six shots," I say.

He begins to smile a little bit. That's when blood rolls out from the back of his head onto the cement. He smiles a little bit more, and before it can wipe away, I make my way up the steps.

I look back. The woman is dead. Children are looking down from the stairway. I take off the medallion and the cape and sink down on the floor next to the wall.

Here comes the sheriff and his deputy. "What have you went and done? You said no more vigilante."

I look down at my side. The shot had gone through the woman and shot my liver out. It is quite painful. The deputy looks at my side, too. "Oh man, that's really bad."

I look up at him. "It's okay. I died long ago." I sink down and die.

Chapter 8
Watch Who You Greet Before You See Who You Meet

Before my first kill, I was scared to death. I cried and shook the whole time. When I first saw him, I walked into the executive building right behind him. I had just gotten my .357 and wanted it for this particular reason.

My stroke of luck. He went straight for the bathroom. I walked in right behind him and put that .357 one inch away from his head while he stood there using the bathroom. I put my thumb on the hammer and began to pull it back.

I couldn't do it. I had ran from fights in the past. I was a little less than a coward then, and now I was a coward again.

I shoved the gun back inside of its holster inside of my vest and turned my back to him. He turned around quickly, glanced at me, and walked straight out of the door.

"Yeah, there ain't no cleaning those hands," I thought. "I'm not through with you yet."

He was the first one to tie me up, and he also tied my ankles up to where if I tried to get away, my ankles would break.

I went home and told the old woman what I had done. "How was it your first time?" I asked her.

"It wasn't easy," she said. "For two weeks, I didn't sleep or eat. The funniest thing though, after two weeks when I did eat, it was over. But the sickness, the nightmares, the sleepless nights. I never got away from those."

But she completed the job.

I didn't.

I was scared.

A coward.

Then, I looked in the paper. Runaways from an orphanage. I was beaten and stabbed before I was cast into the ravine along with my daughter. But this one I remembered. Right before they took me out of the room, the little boy was strapped to the altar for the next initiation.

I remember the sheriff asking me what kind of group it was. Religious, fanatic?

I said, "It was a group. A quest for power."

"Religion, just like I said," the sheriff said.

"Religion, it had nothing to do with religion. They were just cold blooded murderers."

Once somebody gets a belief in their heart, there's no changing it. They believed they were empowered, invincible. If you were able to take a life, so cold and so calculating.

They knew exactly what they were doing.

They were murderers.

Cold blooded murderers.

The old woman told me, "The whole world's full of 'em. If they've got power over you, they feel invincible. They're like wolves traveling in packs, waiting for their next prey. Wolves will kill for sport, too. For the mere practice sake of it. Oh, they eat their prey. They always do. If revenge is what you want," she said, "after you kill that first one, you'll be just like they are. A killer."

She took me ashore again as she had done many times. "I guess I'll see you when you get back." She chuckled under her breath. "That's if you make it back. Revenge has a way of eating at you {til you're all gone." But I knew what she meant. People that set out for revenge often get caught up in its snary web.

They called it Vermont Industries. I spent a lot of time scoping out the area, who went in, who went out. They all went in and out of this building at one time or another one. That's when I saw the young blonde, the one that had pushed the knife into her chest. And I had liked her the most. She was the nicest to my daughter, pretending to love her, to be her best friend.

———————

It was over ten years ago. I had gotten tired of walking with my daughter. She had shopped for a dress and some shoes. I set the bag down beside a stool, a bench, and I sat my weary bones down. I was hardly over my wife's death.

A lady stepped up and sat down on the end of the bench. That's when I met the young blonde. The other woman looked at me. But this was the one that was my fiance', so to speak. "You mind if she sits beside you?" she asked.

As soon as I saw her eyes, I said, "No, I don't mind at all."

"I'm sorry, but shopping is such a handful. We won't be here but a moment."

Her daughter bent over, at least I thought it was her daughter at that time. It was something to do with the latch on her shoe or something. The lady put out her hand. "My name is Delie."

I told her my name as she gave me a firm hand grip. She began to carry on. After a moment of pontificating, she finally asked me, "You come to the mall a lot?"

The one I thought was her daughter raised up. "I love to come to the mall, but I never have anybody to walk with me," she said.

"Now that's not true," the other woman said.

"Except for you, but you get tired too easy," the little blonde answered, signifying her youth and her ability to go farther and longer.

I couldn't disagree. My daughter walked up just then. "Dad, you ready to go?"

The little blonde smiled at her and held out her hand, "Hi, they call me Sara."

My daughter told her her name. "It's nice to meet you," she said. "Dad, come on. I want to go into this shoe store. I wanna show you a cool pair of shoes. They're tennis shoes with heels."

"I'll go with you," the young lady said. "I was wanting to look at shoes before we sat down here."

She turned around and looked at the other lady, "Sure, y'all go ahead. Of course, if that's alright with you," the lady said as she looked at me.

I looked at my daughter. She shrugged her shoulders.

"Okay, I'll be right here when you get back," I said.

Delie was a gasp from the start. She kept looking at me and turning away as if she was trying to keep from... well, to keep from... well, I don't know what she was trying to keep from. It seemed like she was trying to keep from falling for me.

We hit it off right from the start. She kept getting closer and closer. But I couldn't take it anymore. It was time to go. I saw my daughter checking out with the other girl. "Well, I guess it's time for me to go," I said.

She said, "Ahh, just when we were getting to know each other."

"I know, right?"

She looked at me. Her eyes were begging me not to go. "Maybe we'll see you again."

"Maybe," I said.

We had came in on the other end of the mall. The store we came through was closed. Nine o'clock. "Sorry guys, you'll have to go out the main door," the security guard said.

That would mean we would have to walk all the way around, and we did. My daughter didn't say anything else about the scene we had just came out of. I was kinda puzzled myself. Two beautiful women. I didn't ask any questions.

I saw the car far off. Then I saw the blonde walking straight for our car, and then there Delie came from the other side of the department store. She had to go around, too, but apparently, they had gone around the other way. When the young blonde saw my daughter, she looked at her and said, "Are y'all following me?"

The woman met up with me again. "I'm riding with her," she said. "The mall is kind of far, or I would have walked."

I said, "Walking ain't for me. I exercise, but that's enough for me."

She said, "What about the environment? Don't you care about it?"

"I do my part," I said, "but I'm not a fanatic about anything."

She smiled and said, "We're going down to this restaurant to get a bite to eat. Would you and your daughter like to come?"

"No, I'm afraid not. I've really got to go, but it was nice talking to you."

"Well, that's it then. I tried."

"Yeah, you tried," I said, and I laughed about it.

The young blonde looked at us and said, "Ah, you guys." Then she looked at me and said, "Let's ask your daughter. If she wants to, will you come?"

I looked at my daughter. She looked at me. "It's up to you, Dad," she said.

The blonde pulled out two hundred dollars and said, "It's my treat."

"That's a lot of money to be carrying around."

She said, "I make a lot of money."

"Y'all aren't mother and daughter, are you?"

"No, we're just good friends."

"It's really been nice knowing y'all and meeting y'all, but I really have to go," I told them.

The next thing I knew, Delie had her arms wrapped around me and said, "I hope you find what you're looking for."

But all I could think was that if I was looking, I would have just found it. But the fact was I wasn't looking.

I wasn't wanting.

I didn't want her beautiful smile.

I got in the car and drove off. My daughter just kept looking at me. "Daddy! She was beautiful."

"So you liked her, did you?"

After a few facial expressions, she said, "It's been a couple of years. You gotta give somebody a chance."

I said, "I did. I gave you a chance."

"Dad, that's not what I mean."

"I've got all I need," I said.

"You need a wife, and I need a mom."

She was right. I said, "Okay, I'll give it another chance. I'll give it a chance the next time around. "

She told me what restaurant they were going to. "I can't just show up there after I turned 'em down like that," I said.

"It'll be fun, Dad. Come on."

I drove by the restaurant. Their car wasn't there. Easy out. I was so glad. When I got to the house, my emotional state broke down, and so did my daughter's. It was the craziest thing. My cell phone was in my back pocket. When I stood up, I guess I left it there at the mall. The security guard called my daughter's phone number that was on my phone.

"Man, I did not want to go back to the mall," I thought.

"We will be here until ten o'clock," he said. "Much later than that, the main doors will be closed, and you won't be able to get in. You'll have to call me to bring your phone to you."

Ten 'til ten. I left my daughter at the house. The main doors to the entry way of where we were sitting on the bench. When I got there, I had made arrangements to meet him out front.

There she came. She pointed at me and said, "You didn't by any chance leave your phone here, did you?"

I said, "Yeah, how'd you know?"

She said, "I left mine, too, on the bench we were sitting on."

We both began to laugh. I stood there and talked to her for about ten minutes. At ten o'clock, here he came. He walked out the door, pointed at me, and said, "Oh yeah, I'll be right back." When he came back, he had our phones in his hand. He said, "I don't know how you're gonna tell them apart. They're exactly the same. Y'all can figure it out."

He handed my phone to her and her phone to me. As soon as I mashed the button to light up the screen, I knew it was her phone and handed it over to her, saying, "This one's yours."

She was looking straight into my eyes when she took the phone. She said, "Last chance. You wanna go get a drink?"

I felt like there was a frog in my throat. If I could have gotten it up, I would have spit it out, and I couldn't swallow it. The feelings I was starting to have for her were starting to overwhelm me.

She said, "Look, this is my phone number and my address. If you change your mind, call me."

She walked away abruptly then turned around abruptly. "I hope you change your mind," she said with a slight smile on her face as if she was asking again.

I had made up my mind from the time I saw her, but now I

had her information, her phone number, her address. I just couldn't do it. I had already buried one wife. I wasn't about to go through that again. Not under any circumstances. I turned cold and walked away. I got in my car and went back home.

My daughter woke up when she heard me slam the door. It was merely by accident. When I went to shut it, I slipped on the rug that was on the hard wood floor, causing me to slam it. There she was at the top of the stairway.

"Dad, where have you been? It's almost eleven o'clock."

I looked at my watch. It was twenty after eleven. I said, "I'm sorry. I had to go get my phone. It was at the mall."

I told her what had happened. I handed her the phone number. "I have no intentions of calling, you know."

She said, "You don't have to." Then she picked up the phone and called the woman. I tried to get the phone away from her.

My cowardly lion syndrome was at full strength. I was scared to death.

"Hello, this is...,"

After she told her her name, she said, "Look, my dad's a scaredy cat."

I was waving my hands and saying, "No, no," as I whispered in the background. She was saying everything I didn't want her to say and wasn't saying anything that I wanted her to say. If I would have been a cursing man... But I wasn't. I wanted to get mad, but I was scared that I would hurt her feelings.

She stayed on the phone for quite a while. Every word she said, I said, "No, no, no."

"Okay, I'll see you then," she said.

I could have died right there. When she hung up the phone, I couldn't believe it. I rubbed my hand across my forehead and walked the floor. "Why'd you do that?"

"Ah, Dad, you're just a big scaredy cat."

"Of course I'm scared. She's beautiful."

"Yeah...," she said with a big smile on her face. "And what else is she?"

"She's... she's too wonderful. That's what she is." I was dancing in the floor almost. Almost a chilling shiver came over me. I wanted to tell her I was upset, but I was afraid.

"Dad, you need to calm down. She's coming over tomorrow."

I was already dead. "This would have been so much better if you would have let me handle this."

"You did handle it, Dad. I told her it was your idea."

"Did she believe you?"

"No, she called me a liar. Can you believe the nerve of her?"

But I couldn't believe the nerve of my daughter. I was both happy and mad at the same time. Happy because my daughter was finally excited and mad because that's what it took to get her happy. I was tired and full of energy. I was sleepy, but I knew I would get no sleep that night. And I didn't. I tossed and turned. I went into my daughter's room. Three o'clock in the morning.

She raised up on the bed. "Dad, it's gonna be okay."

"Well, I don't feel like it's okay."

"I'll just tell her," I thought. All night long I tossed and turned. "I'll just tell her how I feel. That's all I'll do."

The light was shining through my window. I had been up all night. I had woken my daughter up three or four times. I woke up to the sound of the doorbell. It was eleven thirty.

"He'll be right down," I heard my daughter say. "He's been expecting you."

I thought it was her uncle, an old friend of mine. That's the way she usually acted when he used to come over when my wife was still alive. I came down. There she stood. She wasn't dressed up, but neither was I. I had jogging pants on that I had fallen asleep in and a t-shirt. Could she have caught me at a worse time? I doubt it.

"How did you get my address?"

She said, "I followed you home last night."

"You what?"

"I'm just kidding. Your daughter gave me your address last night on the phone. We're supposed to have lunch. Your daughter said... it was... your idea."

She looked at my daughter and smiled, and that's when I remembered her giving the woman my address. I was shaking like a leaf when she did after I told her not to. Delie could tell I was extremely uncomfortable with the situation. She said, "I can come back later, or not."

I said, "Perhaps later, maybe."

The look on her face reminded me of her, my wife, when they told her she had cancer. She turned to walk away and went for the door.

My daughter said, "Dad!"

I called the lady by her name for the first time. She stopped dead in her steps. I said, "Maybe we could be friends."

She turned around and smiled. "I would really like that."

Chapter 8
Family, Or Not.

The first one I was introduced to after we got to know one another a little bit was a tall good looking man. Executive type, suit, tie. The only time I ever wore a suit was to church. And a tie? Well, every now and then. Banquets, funerals, weddings. And there were very few of those.

He was a very good friend to me. He turned me on to the stocks. I got close to ten thousand dollars when they split.

"You and I are going places," he said.

I had saved up almost six hundred thousand dollars. I trusted him. We had gotten very close. "Trust me," he said. "Take all your money and put it in this stock, and I'll double it over night."

But what he was reluctant to tell me was that he had lost every penny he had just a week before, but he was turned on to a big deal. He would get three times as much. It was an inside thing. He was very convincing.

"I'll give you five hundred thousand," I said.

He said, "No, do the whole thing. I'm good for it. If it falls through, I'll pay you back myself."

He showed me his checking account. It ran in the millions, and in the zeroes, and then back into the millions.

I told him I didn't doubt his veracity. "But this is my daughter's college money," I said.

I wrote out a check and said, "I'm gonna trust you on this."

Meanwhile, I had been dating the woman I thought I was gonna marry. Every weekend, my daughter... It started out one young blonde, and then two, and then three.

My daughter's killer was told, "The kill doesn't count unless you're intimate with your prey. It's easy to kill someone you don't know, but killing someone you care about, that kind of strength commands dedication, commitment. Only then can one be empowered."

The young blonde asked, "What is the empowerment?"

"The strength to do anything. The power to change the outcome of anything you run across."

"But I already have that power," she said.

"But not like you will."

Still not fully convinced, that's when a check was written out to me. My good friend handed me a million dollar check. "I'm sorry it didn't make as much as I thought it would," he said, but the plain out fact was that he had made ten times that amount on that money.

But now he had my full trust. I would have trusted him with anything now. A million dollars. He could have taken my six hundred thousand and ran. He had access to my bank, my house, my cars, everything. When I got back to my house, it was no longer my house.

The killer of my daughter, they possessed everything their prey owned. My checking account was cleaned out and closed. Online checking, it's the greatest. If you're a thief.

By the way, he made up for the two hundred thousand that he owed me. He paid for everything. We went on the most exotic vacations, jungle safaris, anything you could imagine. They even tried to get me to go rhino hunting, but I was scared to death. I stayed in the car, only to have a rhino hit right in front of my knee where I was at in the back seat. The driver's door wouldn't open after that. And guess who the driver was.

Old Fearless.

Nina.

My first kiss with Delie. I was so in love. I was in love before, but not like this. It was different. She had completely mesmerized me. She was perfect in everything she said, everything she did. She found a wounded dog and took it to the vet. She was full of compassion and love. I could not even believe that one time earlier on that she had her initiation.

Hypocrites.

Liers in wait.

Sheep.

Wolves on the inside.

Mama always told me about being wary of sheep in wolves' clothing, but she never prepared me for sheep with wolves inside of them.

She never told me she loved me. I never told her. But I could see it just as plain as day. She was in love with me. I shed not a tear when I stood over her dead body. I gasped for air, just like she was a gasp for me.

My dearest, best friends.

All twelve of them.

All the way up to what I thought was the top.

It wasn't even the start.

"She'll be the end of me," I said to my daughter. "I know it."

"Why, Dad? 'Cause you're so afraid of falling in love?"

"That fear's long past."

"Really, Dad?"

"I'm afraid so."

"You're thinking of getting married?"

"I'm afraid so."

She smiled. "We have such wonderful friends now. They do everything for us."

The executive came back to me. We played pool together. We bowled. We were all such great friends. Every week, we did something different. More extraordinary than the last. Ice skating, sky diving, mountain climbing, scuba diving, fishing trips, sometimes for weeks at a time. We all went on cruises.

But it was him that I stopped at, unable to shoot him in the back of the head. Because I was a coward. I was scared.

"Another girl disappeared from the orphanage," the old woman had said.

"Where did you get the paper?" I looked at the date. It was three months old.

She said, "I don't buy the paper. I'm sure you know that by now."

Yeah, I knew it. But she did take fish to the market, and they would give her a stack of old newspapers so she could wrap 'em up in it.

That's when I read another one and another one. Then, I thought about him again. And I thought about it again after I stood over his dead body.

"You took everything from me," I stood over him and said. "You took everything. You left me nothing."

But something came over me. The head master was right. There was an empowerment after you killed somebody. It was a power like I had never known.

I went on to the next one. She had completely won my daughter's heart. She was beautiful spirited. She came over every day. She helped with school work, house work. It finally got to the point where we gathered there at the house at least once in the afternoon after everybody got off of work, making big plans.

"We could go take a ride on a space shuttle for a hundred thousand dollars a piece," the little blonde said.

I was quick to speak up. "I don't wanna ride on a space shuttle. I like gravity. Anything outside of that, there's a reason for it."

"Mr. Hourson, there's still gravity out in outer space."

"I like the kind that keeps my feet on the ground, not the kind that pulls me away to another planet."

"Oh Daddy, I'd like to go."

"Mr. Hourson, I'll pay for it if you let her go."

"Exactly what does it do?"

"It takes off in a rocket. Once it reaches the outer atmosphere, we get to take pictures, video, and for a million dollars, we get to fly around the whole Earth as fast as the Earth rotates."

"Well, maybe y'all could fly around it backward and gain a day."

My daughter jumped up and down. She was very excited. "Does that mean I get to go?"

"Let's all go," my girlfriend said.

I was usually game for about anything, as long as it didn't concern leaving the house. But wasting my money wasn't one of 'em, and that was expensive. But as usual, I got dragged along with my gullible state of mind. I didn't care anything about space or space ships. I didn't even like airplanes, but they had talked me into sky diving.

They did it all day. I did it one time. "No thanks, I'll keep my feet on the ground."

"Oh go on, you big ol' chicken," my girlfriend said. "Jump out, and pull the chute cord."

"You mean the rip cord?"

Then she pushed me, and right out the plane I went. I was spinning and turning in every direction, but I remembered what the instructor said. "Put your hands and feet out straight. Bend 'em back slightly. When you get leveled out and you feel comfortable, pull the chute."

I could have died when I didn't see the rip cord. I was frantic. I was scared.

I was scared of everything.

I was scared I was gonna be late to work.

 I was scared I was gonna lose my money.

I was scared I was gonna lose the most important thing to me, my daughter.

But I didn't want gravity to be the thing that took it.

Here came my girlfriend. She grabbed me in midair. "You okay?" she screamed out at the top of her lungs.

I shook my head no. She reached down, pulled the cord, and then disappeared. About ten seconds later, I finally was able to open my eyes just a little bit to look down, and on top of her parachute I was. She was about a hundred yards below me. Then I saw her parachute fold up, and I came right down in the middle of it, right onto the ground.

My girlfriend got up, took her helmet off, and came over, jumping up and down. "That was great!"

"I thought you were an environmentalist."

"Very much so," she said.

"Well, this doesn't seem like much use for the environment."

She said, "No, but it sure was fun. Let's do it again."

"If you can get me up in a plane again, have at it, but my feet are staying on the ground from now on."

She grabbed me briskly for a moment with her hands around

my shoulders and neck. "You don't have to be scared of everything. You need empowerment."

"The last thing I want is empowerment."

She said, "I'm not talking about a booster drink."

But now I understand what she was talking about.

"I can't do it," I said. "I can't keep up with you guys. Next thing you know, you'll be on the moon."

She said, "I don't understand. Usually when people sky dive for the first time, they usually don't have a fear of anything else after that."

"It doesn't seem logical to me," I said. "Fear's kept me alive this long, and I don't mind being a fraidy cat."

She said, "Maybe that's why I love you so much." She was so convincing.

I stood over her dead body.

A million things ran through my heart.

A million things pierced my soul.

For God's sake why didn't I feel anything? I couldn't even cry. Scared? You were right, I should have told her. Once something empowers you, you're not afraid of anything."

There I was, a cold blooded killer with no heart, no feelings. Empathy died a long time ago. The very thing she called fear was the very thing I called reverence. Respect.

But her little friend, the one I shot at her vanity, she was so nice to my daughter. I woke up briefly after my daughter was dead, hanging there, broken ankles. I was barely alive. Blood oozing out of the wound that they obviously gave me while I was passed out, thinking I was dead.

She removed her hood as she looked at my face and then looked down. That's when I opened my eyes. There was empathy I saw. I could tell she didn't want to be there. She looked up over at my daughter as they removed her body, preparing hers. She was next in line. They cut the bands off my ankles. I passed out again.

I woke up another brief moment just to hear the one with the BMW say, "I wish you could have joined us, old friend. I really liked you."

But he was right. I should have joined 'em, long ago. That way I could have known precisely who I was gonna kill.

Vigilante.

I think not.

Revenge.

Not a chance.

I was a superhero.

Invincible.

Empowered.

Just like my girlfriend said. Once you feel the power, you won't fear anything. But there was no fear, no agonizing pain of defeat. But the fear wasn't all that was gone. There was nothing.

———————

My daughter's eighth birthday. The kitchen light went out. "Honey, can you change the light bulb?"

"Heavens no, call the electrician. You want me to get electrocuted?"

"Don't be silly. It's just a light bulb. You can stand on a chair and just reach it."

"I'm not quite tall enough."

I was a little boy when my cousin went to reach up to unscrew a light bulb. The switch was still on. I heard somebody go, "Uuhh." When I went into the bedroom, there he laid on the floor. The bulb had busted while he was trying to change it. His hand went into the filament. No, he wasn't dead, but it scared me so bad that terror terrified my life afterward. I was afraid of everything.

I wouldn't go into a dark room.

I wouldn't go into a basement.

I wouldn't go into an attic.

I went to church and did everything I knew to do that was right. The preacher said, "You shouldn't fear like that."

I said, "But fear is the beginning of wisdom."

"Mr. Hourson, the fear of God is the beginning of wisdom. Fear is of demonic forces."

I only knew that too well when he invited me back to church. "It's been a long time, old friend. We miss you."

But church was over with.

My daughter was fixing to turn nine. We went on a vacation. Caverns. "This is the hole in the wall. New Mexico. These caverns have been developing over eons of time. Some of 'em even millions of years old," he said.

We were all ready to take the tour when the guide said, "We've only lost two people on these tours, but they were never found again. Y'all stick close. There are hundreds of passages. You venture off..."

He was trying to sound scary, but I began to shake. I was literally afraid of everything. I grabbed my daughter's hand. "No, we're not going in there."

"But Dad..."

I looked into her eyes. "I can't do it."

"Then let me. I can."

And she did. She took beautiful pictures while she was in there. The whole time we were on our way back to the house, I regretted that I didn't go. She named about thirty different rocks. She had a great time. I was miserable.

"Oh God, if only I was just not a coward, not afraid to do everything."

But after my wife died, things changed drastically for me. I quit being afraid as much, but I quit doing everything. Especially after the vacation. My daughter could get me to go to the mall once a month, and that was about it. I protected her so much.

———————

And now this little blonde. I watched her for a while. I was like a monster when she saw me. She wouldn't even turn around, but all I could think was, "Where's your empowerment? Where's your strength? Where's your no fear of dying?"

Terror ripped across her face. As I looked in the mirror, half of her face disappeared, the way she should have looked.

But it was only the next thing, the next one on the altar. She got up on the little boy and sat on his stomach, and as the other girl had done to my daughter, a christening, another empowerment. She cried the whole time she pushed the dagger into his chest.

But when she pulled it out, her full cup was empty. Her warm heart was cold. This wasn't empowerment. This was death. Not for the victim, but the stalker. This one wouldn't sleep or eat right after this deal because she genuinely liked me and my daughter, and so did my so called girlfriend.

Chapter 9
Dark Hour

It was only after the twelfth one, after I knew they were dead, I laid my pistol down. I didn't file the serial numbers. I didn't clean the fingerprints off the cartridges or the gun. I made sure there were good clean fingerprints on every cartridge. Yeah, I thought about finishing myself. But there were others, and they needed to be taken care of, too.

From day one, the old lady showed me what to do. She helped me do the investigating. "Oh yeah, this goes real high up," she said. "Executives, city officials, professors, maybe even higher, but they're stemming from the college. The woman in charge there. She's not a good person."

I said, "Are you kidding? None of them are good people."

She said, "But she's really bad. You'll have to be careful with her. She's a sly one."

We made careful plans. "You've gotta make sure it ain't revenge. It'll swallow you whole. I spoke to a pawn shop owner. Here's two hundred and sixty dollars. Put the gun in your name.

Make everything legal."

"But they'll know I'm alive then. I don't want that."

"He's not gonna turn in the paperwork 'til the time comes."

"And what time will that be?"

She handed me the list. "When he sees the twelfth name in the newspaper and knows they're dead, he's gonna release the paperwork."

And that's just what he did. As soon as the paperwork hit the internet, the government database kicked in. The serial numbers popped in and identified the gun and the new address that I had. After I left the building where I lived, I went back and got my job back. That's how I made my money.

It was the detective. "This one's gonna be a hard one," she said. "You won't be able to kill him without being charged."

"Then how am I gonna get to him?" I asked her.

"Don't worry. I've made arrangements with an old cop friend. Whatever you do, don't trust anybody in the sheriff's department. To get in there, you'll have to be arrested. Maybe even turn yourself in. I know the sheriff. He's a good guy. But after you're in, this is what you'll have to do..."

After carefully explaining every detail, that's when the old woman told me, "I'll never kill again. I made an oath to myself. I've helped you all I can, up to the point of *killing*."

———————

It was the one in charge at the college. She was talking to the dean. "More recruits. A man and his daughter. Pretty soon, we'll have the whole city rumbling after what we have. They'll pay

83

plenty for the empowerment."

He smiled, and she smiled back at him. She had talked to my daughter about college. She was one of the friends. She was very close. "Yes, this will be a great college for you."

She had talked to her about classes, when she would start. My daughter was a straight A student. She had pulled some strings. "When you're fourteen, you can take this test. If you pass it, we can get you straight into college."

My daughter would've done anything any one of them would have said, but it was the twenty something year old boy. She had fallen in love with him. I found out from her journal she left open one day when she went to school. "I'm an so in love with..."

When I saw that, that's when I ended the mall going. "No more. You're just a little girl. You don't know what you're getting into."

"Daddy, you're afraid of everything. I know what I'm doing."

"I know what I'm doing, too."

The little blonde showed up again. I said, "No more. You're too old for her, and your boyfriend and these other boys are too old for her, too. The influence is wrong."

"Now don't be like that, Mr. Hourson. You know how your fear is."

That's when my girlfriend laid it on thick. "There's a way to get rid of that fear."

One by one, they entered into the house. My decision would prove my fatality. "We're an elite group," my girlfriend said. "Us twelve. We're all in twelves. There are two christenings going to happen pretty soon. We want you and your daughter to join the christening. I love you," she said. "Please, it's for our... it's for our..." She stumbled on words. She couldn't even say it.

"For the good? Is that the word you're trying to spit out?"

She gave me a hurt look.

"So what is the empowerment? What are y'all? Some kinda cult?"

"Not at all," she said. "We believe in the good. That's what we do. We do good for everybody. We purge the system," she said. "That's what I am, an environmentalist. I do what's good for the environment."

"Yeah, it's like picking weeds out of a garden, ain't it? So what is the empowerment?"

"The power to take a life."

"What?!?! You took a life?!?!"

"It was the only way," she cried.

They all said it was the only way.

My daughter looked at 'em, shaking her head no. I said, "There's no way I'm taking a life. There's no way I'm a killer. I'll never join your group."

My daughter's eyes got big. The only time I had ever stood up in my whole life. Twelve monsters.

"Please won't you reconsider."

"Not if my life depended on it."

The head master said, "What about your daughter's life? What if it depended on that?"

"Is that a threat? Y'all are all my friends. You're gonna turn against me?"

"There's no other way," the head master said. "You're either with us one hundred percent, or you're not with us at all."

"Get out of my house! And don't ever come back!"

"So that's it then? That's your final answer."

"This ain't no game show. You're talking about innocent lives."

He laughed. "Innocent? We're purging the world. The homeless, the weak, the poor, the unwanted."

"You can put me on that list because I'm never gonna do what y'all do. Y'all are nothing but murderers."

His eyes got big. I knew I was in trouble. There was no turning back now. I had went too far. I should have played along with 'em, but I wasn't very smart. I shouldn't have let fear make my decision. I was careless.

The old woman said, "It's not gonna be easy."

But when I shot him, the young man my daughter had a crush on, I had mercy.

She had come to him, the one at the college. "You'll be rich," she said.

"But I'm already rich. My parents are rich. Their parents were rich before them."

"Rich in power," she said.

"What do I need with power? I've got money. That is power."

"You'll have money like you've never seen." She was very convincing. "And the power you'll feel, you'll feel the invincibility of being able to do anything."

She had conned all the young ones into it. The more pride of riches they had, the easier it was to convince 'em. The ones that didn't get convinced disappeared. You had one chance in, and no chance out. You either killed, or you were the sacrifice. The one time kill. There for a while, they couldn't get any new recruits. They became nothing more than cold blooded murderers, killing anybody that didn't convert.

The head master said, "This is your last chance. When we walk out that door, that will be the end of it."

"You're a liar." My somewhat fear died when I saw the terror on my shaking little girl's face. She was in shock.

"You're right. I am a liar. If you're not for us, then you're against us."

The men tried to grab me. I hit anything I could. My fist hit my girlfriend's face. I knocked her completely out. I was aiming for the guy that grabbed my arm. That's when the lights went out, right in the back of the head. I woke up twice on the way there, but I was so dazed and confused I had forgotten about it.

I heard the guy with the BMW say, "Let's give 'em another chance. I really like these guys."

The head master said, "They must die. They know too much."

But I didn't know anything at all. I had no idea about the killings, the murders they had committed. I wasn't even fully convinced that they were not kidding, until I saw the look on my daughter's face.

She stayed in shock 'til the dagger went into her chest, about an inch at first, when she began to cry out, "Daddy!"

The little blonde, Nina, raged, "Go on! Do it!"

Sara made sure she suffered, pushing the knife in very slowly. The head master convinced her. "The slower the death, the longer the suffering, and the stronger you'll be."

The little blonde shook horribly as she sat on my daughter's belly and pushed the dagger into her chest. I groaned.

When I took my first step, it was a long time after the old woman had found me.

"They call it hobbling," she said.

"What do you mean, hobbling?"

"Because once your ankles are broken this way, you can only hobble around. They used to put two by fours in between the legs at the lower part and take sledge hammers and beat inwardly, breaking both ankles."

I said, "That ain't what happened in this case."

"It was arranged the same way. Hobbling comes in different forms and is created different ways."

"How long will I hobble?"

"You'll never walk again, not the same way. The bones never mend the same. Your ankles are crooked, and I don't have the means to set 'em, either one of 'em."

"You mean they're gonna have to be broken again?"

"You'll have to have surgery," she said. "There ain't no other way. Modern times ain't like they used to be. Cripples stayed cripples back then, but this can be fixed now."

But I couldn't stop thinking about the blonde, Nina. She was so cold and so energetic. She acted like she was on steroids constantly. This one stayed mad at me a lot. "You're such a party pooper."

"Party pooper? Are you kidding me? I do everything you guys say and want to do."

"You don't do everything with us. You're scared of everything. You need empowerment. You need to be free. Like me. Free to *kill* time."

But it was the way she said *kill*. I was afraid of her. She was all the time rubbing herself on me and petting me and rubbing her hands through my hair.

My girlfriend called her down a couple of times. "Okay, that's enough, Nina. Get your own boyfriend," she said with a smile.

"But he's so good looking," Nina said.

The fact was I was scared to death of her. It was her moral standard. Out in society, she walked the chalk line, but when she was with me, she was under dressed, overactive. Fast cars, fast life, and spent a lot of money. I stopped letting my daughter go anywhere with her.

"How come you're so afraid of me?"

"Afraid of you? I'm not afraid of you. I'm horrified of you, and you know why."

She laughed. "You're afraid of everything."

I came home early from work one day, and there she was in the living room.

"Where's your car at?"

"In the backyard."

"What are you sneaking around here for?"

"I was waiting for you."

"No, you weren't waiting for me. I've got a girlfriend."

She got a little more revealing, you know the type. "I know you have a girlfriend, and I'm okay with that. You can keep your girlfriend," she said as she slid her arms around my neck. "You can have anything you want, anytime you want."

"I've got everything I want." I pulled her arms down from around my neck 'til they were in front of us.

She put her hands on my chest and pushed me back a little bit. She turned around and flipped her hair back a little bit. "Oh well, you can't blame a girl for trying." She put her back up against my chest and looked up at me.

"She's your friend. Why would you betray her?" I asked her.

"We don't betray one another. We encourage one another." She pulled my arms around her belly. "Don't be afraid!"

But I couldn't help but to shake. She was more enticing, and I was so gullible. Before I even knew what happened, she was out the door and I was left on the couch, crying my eyes out. You can't imagine how I felt about her. I was torn one way and scared to death the other.

My girlfriend walked in the door. "Couldn't you have gotten here a little sooner?" I thought.

"Honey, what's wrong?"

"Nothing."

Her eyes got big. My answer was blunt and painful.

"Nina was here, wasn't she?"

My eyes got real big.

"She seduced you, didn't she?"

She smiled.

I broke down and cried.

"It's okay," she told me.

"What?!? What'd you say?"

She said, "It's okay."

"You're okay with that?" I asked.

"I love you," she said. "I don't mind sharing."

"What?!?!?" I put my hand on my ears. "I'm not marrying this woman," I thought to myself.

That's when things started to go down hill. Each one of 'em, the little dark secret was revealed.

The twenty girl year old guy got to my now thirteen year old daughter's heart. I asked him, "What are your intentions?"

"Nothing right now."

"Okay, what are your intentions later?"

"I won't do anything without your approval," he said. "That I promise you."

It was the first time I woke up. "You...you...you promised you wouldn't hurt her."

But he just looked at me, and I passed back out.

Now the BMW, I really liked that car, but ever so often when I drove by a certain motel, I saw one just like it. But after the two or three incidents went on, this particular day, I saw the car there.

The top was on it, which was unusual. But as I drove by, I saw him get out of the car.

I turned around, pulled into the quite expensive little motel, and lowered down the window on the passenger's side. "What are you doing here?"

He looked up at a room. So did I. That's when I saw the curtain open when I looked back up there. All I saw was blonde hair.

I said, "Never mind."

"You won't tell, will you? This wasn't my idea."

Nina.

Once you were in the clique, you had to do whatever you were beckoned to do.

"Tell who? I don't know your wife and kids. You've never brought 'em to my house." I looked back up there. "Besides, this is your affair, not mine."

But he didn't go back up to the room. He got in his car, shaking his head. "No more. This will never happen again."

But if it was Nina, I knew it would happen again if she wanted it to. She was enticing. She was beautiful. And she got what she wanted when she wanted it. She was nothing more than a rich spoiled little girl that needed serious correction. Encouraging people to do wrong. Using her influence like it was a sexual orientation.

But I couldn't help it. I was scared to death of her because she pulled at my heart so hard. "Kill her!" she said while the girl was on top of my daughter.

I tilted my head to the side, watching Nina bleed out. Her

beautiful young body laying there in the shower. I should have felt something. But I couldn't feel anything. I was cold. I wanted to be happy that she was groaning in agonizing pain. For forty-five minutes, she bled just a little bit at a time. She kept looking at me.

I tilted my head to the other side and said, "Encouraged? Are you encouraged now?"

Forty-five minutes I stood there. I reached up and turned the water off. A clear red line ran down to the drain. I knelt down and touched the bottom of her foot and slowly looked up 'til I saw the wound and slowly moved my eyes upward, watching her breathe each breath, and then I looked into her eyes.

All she did was stare at me while I looked into her eyes deeply while she looked back as if she didn't recognize me with fear in her eyes.

A fear I had never seen in Nina.

"So you are afraid?" I asked her.

Her eyes widened just a little bit, puzzled at what I said as if she didn't know what I was talking about.

Forty minutes later, I clicked the hammer back again. Her eyes got wide just one more time. It looked like she was beginning to say something.

Such a waste.

I hate waste.

This one was wasteful.

She wasted her life.

"Riches. There's your riches. I hope you can take 'em with you," I said.

Chapter 10
There's No Turning Back

But it is when I was shot at the orphanage. I am laying there. My heart has stopped, but I can still hear. All of the sudden, part of the sheriff's head flies completely apart. Then I hear a voice that sounds familiar.

"Hold it right there, Deputy. You in with it?"

"No, I ain't in with it. I ain't in with nothing," he says.

"Did you know he was the ring leader? He almost pulled it off."

"Who are you?"

"That's my dad laying there."

But it can't be. I can still hear. But how can it be? I watched her stabbed into the heart.

"But you're dead," the deputy says.

She says, "I've been dead for over ten years. I woke up two cities over. They drug me out of a ravine. How I was even alive, they didn't even know. The puncture in my chest completely missed my heart. I didn't remember anything for years. 'Til I saw these last killings in the paper, and I saw my dad's name, arrested for murder. It wasn't until I saw his name that I remembered everything."

"You're under arrest," he says to her.

The fact is, it is my daughter. But it isn't the one that was sacrificed. She is lying. It was before I got married. I had not even known about her until after I had my other kid. But she knew about me. She fills the deputy in while she points the gun at him.

"You mean to tell me he didn't even know he had another daughter?"

But yet I lay here. My heart doesn't pump not one bit of blood. The warm blood oozes out of my cold body. She stands there looking over me.

"There's nothing you can do for him now. That's dark red blood," the deputy says.

She points the gun at him, right at his head. "If he dies, so will you."

"Ma'am, he's already dead."

She clicks the hammer back once, and then she clicks it back real slow 'til it clicks again. He grabs my body and pulls it away from the wall. I am lying flat in a puddle of blood. He looks at the wound, and as quick as he can, he takes his shirt off, wraps it around my waist, pulls it as tight as he can, and begins to bang on my chest.

I wake up in intensive care, and there she stands over me. I have tubes down my throat, in my nose, out of my arms, probes hooked to my temples, my chest. There is blood going in, liquid coming out of tubes out of my stomach. I look like something out of a horror flick. The first thing that comes out is the tube out of my throat.

"Are you my daughter?" I ask her.

"Heavens no, I'm a nurse. Can't you tell by the uniform?"

"Where's my daughter at?"

"Hon, you better wait here and let me go get the doctor."

The doctor comes in. First thing he does is look at the chart. "Significant changes for the good. I'm surprised you made it at all."

"But I died."

"Nah, you didn't die," he smiles and says, "but it was close."

"Where's the sheriff?"

"Well, I don't rightly know where the sheriff is. You didn't come here with the sheriff."

"Well, how did I get here?" I ask, still barely able to talk.

"Well, you came in an ambulance."

"What about my daughter?"

"Sir, you didn't come here with your daughter. You came by yourself. Maybe you can call her on the phone."

But I don't know her number, and I don't know who to call. There is one number I do remember. But she is dead. I let go of the phone while it's still in his hand.

"I heard my daughter shoot the sheriff," I say.

The sheriff walks in. "There he is," he says.

I look at him astonished. "You're the ring leader. My daughter shot you in the head."

"Now, Mr. Hourson, do I look like I'm shot in the head? And

you know I ain't the ring leader."

"But when I was laying there, my daughter came in and shot you and said you were the ring leader."

The doctor says, "You lost a lot of blood. You were probably hallucinating."

"Is that possible? It seemed so real. I had a daughter out of wedlock."

"Morphine."

"But I hadn't had morphine when I was dead, when my heart stopped."

"Mr. Hourson, you never died. If your heart would have stopped, you wouldn't be here."

The sheriff looks at me. "You got some imagination. Now you told me you wouldn't do no more vigilante work."

"I didn't. I went there to get information, and that ain't where it started from. That was just a part of their operation for their sacrifices."

I am hardly able to talk.

"Here, Mr. Hourson, have some water."

"The college," I tell them.

"I knew it," the deputy says. "I knew it."

The sheriff says, "Don't you worry. We got it under control."

Now I end up laying in that hospital for a long, long time, and during that process, the sheriff, FBI, homicide, they get to the bottom of the whole racketeering operation.

The dean, he had started the whole empowerment thing in this city. It was the rich kids that he was attacking. "Oh yes, once you're empowered..." He was nothing more than a con and a liar.

He no more believed what he was saying than a poor man had a mansion, if that even makes any sense at all.

It is almost six weeks before I get out of the hospital. They have to redo my insides or something. A bunch of my insides are cut out for the damage. I have a severe stomach ache for almost a year, but it is the day I get out of the hospital. The sheriff comes to pick me up.

"I could charge you for murder," he says.

"No you can't. It's because of me that the investigation has ended, and you won't get all the glory for it. Where's the other sheriff?"

"In Honolulu, happily retired."

"When did that occur?"

"Well, it didn't happen like you said it would happen, but it was pretty close. Mr. Hourson, you better stay out of trouble now." He shakes my hand and walks away.

But I am no vigilante.

I'm a killer.

Chapter 11
I Feel Nothing

Nina was impossible. She went from one person to the next, trying to spark a new life, a new event. Whatever got her heart pumping the most. She was fearless alright. She just hadn't felt the pain that I felt.

"It's okay," she said. "We all share."

But I didn't wanna share. I didn't want her at all. None of us did. We felt sorry for her. But she was like a plague of personality. I was nothing but putty in her hands. Gullible and scared to say no.

I told my girlfriend, "This ain't the way it should be."

She said it was alright again, trying to ease the guilt and the pain."All you need is just a little encouragement, and there are ways to get courage." She smiled with irony on her face, but I just blew her off and quickly changed the subject.

The old woman spent eight years helping me set things up.

The last warning she gave me was, "Look out for the detective. I don't know how he's in there, but he's in tight. He can't be touched."

She helped me set the details of it up, planning. "I don't much care about revenge," she said. "It ate up thirty years of my life, but I'll spend my dying day helping you get rid of these guys. Murderers, they ain't met a killer yet. I used to be a real cold one," she said as she stared off with anger on her face and an interrogating look as she breathed deep and heavy. She looked at me and said, "I ain't much warmed up to anything until I run into you."

She looked at me with an earnest look like she had held back her behavior or something. "You won't have to get him. It'll have to be inside. But I already got it planned. When your paperwork shows up, I've been sneaking a little information out of your paperwork, like the disappearance of you and your daughter."

But she wouldn't give me the piece that was missing. I asked her repeatedly. "What did it say?"

"You wouldn't wanna see it anyway," she said. "Just leave it at that."

She cried a little bit.

"Killer," I thought, "well, you're as soft as I am."

I didn't put two and two together 'til the sheriff and his deputy told me they'd found my daughter's body years ago. "Yeah, nobody would have recognized her. We labeled her as Jane Doe."

She had spared me the pain, but the sheriff, he laid it on thick. "Didn't have a drop of blood in her body, cut off the palms of her hands all the way to each fingertip. The same thing with her feet.

Pulled all her teeth—"

That's when I had said, "I don't wanna hear anymore."

"After they mangled her face up," he kept going.

He looked at me with tears in his eyes. He was beginning to understand. I asked him, "Why would they do such a thing? She was already dead."

He said, "Well, I'll tell you why. 'Cause we couldn't identify the body. With no blood type, we couldn't even sum it down to a few, and without you reporting her missing or somebody reporting y'all missing... We found a bunch of children like this through the years, if we found 'em at all. We also found a little boy like that."

That was no doubt the next sacrifice the night I was there.

After I saw the boy, BMW stood over me, watching me bleed out. He was the fusser. "I always get stuck with clean up," he said.

The other guy said, "You're the strongest here. Why wouldn't you?"

"I ruined a two thousand dollar suit last time."

"That's why we wear these capes."

"Yeah, well, I'm not taking it off til I'm finished this time."

Out I went again.

―――――――――

But I felt the power like I'd never felt it, and I had no sense of emotion the whole time the sheriff had spoke to me.

"Afraid you said? I can't believe you were afraid of anything ever. Unless this whole thing's went to your head, and you began to believe what they taught you." He laughed and said, "I just don't believe it."

Every time he went out of the room Friday, he came back and said, "Everything you said pans out."

But it was the detective going to the D.A. "Let me do the interrogation."

"The sheriff's handling the investigation. He's getting the low down on just about everybody involved."

"Involved in what? It's an open and close case."

"What's the matter, Detective? You afraid the sheriff's gonna get one of your killing points? He said it would be closed by Friday. If it ain't, then I'll send you in, but until then..."

That's when he handed him a folder. "Explain why these two ended up dead. Just like on all your cases."

"They were shooting at me."

But he had lost three partners through the years. Lying about each one of them. But this last one... The D.A. didn't trust him, and the sheriff had his suspicion.

"We'll get to the bottom of all this, but you stay out of the sheriff's way until we do," the D.A. told him.

But it was two years earlier. The old woman speaking to the D.A. "I got some information," she said. "On one of your detectives."

She filled him in. He wrote everything on a clipboard and then tore the piece of paper off and said, "I'll get this to whom it may concern."

But it wasn't long after that when she died. She had made it back just in time. She grabbed me by the hand. "I've done all I can for you, but don't you forget about that detective. He's dirty. He's kept his hands clean up 'til now, but he's getting careless. Oh yeah.. that D.A.," she shook her head, "he ain't what he..."

"What? What did you say?"

She just looked at me, but I could only guess at what she was gonna say. "He ain't cut out to what he's supposed to be."

It was poison. It was only when she folded over in front of me that I saw the little mark. Her old gray hair pulled to the side. You would've hardly noticed. It was almost like a mosquito bite. Maybe just a little bigger. She died of a heart attack alright. That's what the poison did. It stopped her heart. It was a wonder she made it as far as she did. They thought that they had missed her.

The poor thing had banged on her chest the whole time she rowed her boat across the water. "I've gotta warn him about that D.A. Come on, old heart. Come on, old heart," she said as she hit herself repeatedly in the middle of the chest.

I rolled her back over. She had a big smile on her face. She knew now that I was prepared and knew what to deal with. I burnt her old house down with her in it. I took the old boat and left.

———————

I could hear the sheriff again. "Don't go taking the law into your own hands again. Up 'til now, nobody knows you but me, and I know what you've done."

"What about your deputy?"

"I don't know why he likes you, but he does. He don't like too many people."

But that was a long time ago, and the old woman didn't tell me how to plan for this. I have been watching him, the D.A., for three months now. It is the first girl I see him with.

It's Nina.

I'm in shock.

How?

She hugs and kisses him, but there is something different about her. How is she doing it? How could she have done it? She couldn't have. She couldn't have lived.

Her exact persona.

The way she touched a man, leaving her middle finger the last thing she touched as she would roll her hand down gently off their skin, their face, their arm.

I follow her around a few days, too. The college. Two more blondes. Now there are three colleges. Highly respected. I find ten of 'em. But it it's the D.A. that I'm after.

But it is that night. I follow him to a building. I try everything I know to get into it, and here comes the Nina look alike. Head all up in the air. All full of herself.

I purchased a piece of land. It took me a while. But I have a bunker underground. I'm debating. If I take her tonight, it will be quick and easy. But I know her personality. She will never know I'm here.

It is the back door in the alley way, I have been observing it, and Nina is the last one in when I put the cards in the door. The door closes quickly, but it doesn't come all the way closed. She is careless.

I don't have my gun, but I have not planned on killing

anybody tonight either. But it is initiation night. I follow her 'til I can't follow her anymore. She goes down an elevator. I go down the steps. She goes down a long hall, and from the basement level, she goes downward again.

There they are, in their cloaks again. I see the Nina look alike in the back room. I ponder for a moment, staring at her naked body as she slips into a black cloak. She looks at me and pulls her hand through her hair. She smiles a little bit as she pulls up her cloak slowly.

I walk in very slowly. I can see what she is thinking, "Fresh meat. A newcomer."

"I didn't know we were going to have two christenings tonight," she says.

I pick up one of the black cloaks and slide it over my clothes. She says, "It's easier to get the blood off if you don't have your clothes on underneath."

I smile. She shrugs her shoulders and goes on out. "I'll see you later," she says.

"Where's the D.A.?"

"Oh, he'll be here. He doesn't miss these for anything, and you aren't supposed to use titles around here."

As soon as I get out of that room, she pushes me in front of all of 'em. "Here's our newcomer. He oughta go first."

But the one in charge looks at Nina. "You know the rules, Nina."

The fact is, I'm in shock. I'm caught red handed. "He'll have to come to the next christening," he says. But I was even more shocked when he said Nina.

It's another little girl. She is nine. The boy is nineteen. He is eager to go. "Hurry up, let's get this over with!"

Finally, I hear his voice. It's the district attorney.

"Nina, what's next?" I ask her.

"My name's not Nina."

"I heard 'em call you Nina."

"We aren't supposed to use names, but my name is Hazel."

But when they bring the little girl out, I look for an instrument, a killing device. All I can see is a flag pole with an empowerment banner on it. The all too eager boy gets up on top of the little girl. I am fixing to run, but I hear the D.A.'s voice again.

The boy lifts up the dagger to jab it into the young girl when the D.A. yells, "No! Empathy! Without empathy, you cannot possess the power."

"But I know her. I know her whole family."

She begs him. "Please don't kill me!"

He lifts up the dagger again. Still unable to push it through slow. Torture. There is that voice again.

"I can do it," he says. "Just give me a little time."

One of the other blondes grabs his hand. "You must do it slow and gentle. She must feel the pain so that you won't."

"I can't do it," he says. "I can't kill nobody. I'm not a killer. I never was a killer. I never wanted to kill nobody. I thought this was all a joke. I was just going along with all of y'all."

"You were at the last christening. You knew what to expect. Now you must pay the price."

"No! I can do it. Hold on! I know I can."

Then, he goes upright. The D.A. has just stabbed him in the back. "It looks like the new guy's in for a treat. He gets to do the christening instead."

He pulls the cloak off of my head. "This is it," I think.

That's when a red light on the ceiling starts going around. "Grab the girl," he says, speaking to me. "We got a back way out."

I grab the girl as quick as I can. I wrap the cloak around her, and I follow 'em down a secret entry that closes after we go through. I follow 'em closely until they get to where there is an exit. It is a man hole two blocks from where the building is, in a back alley. I stay back for a moment, watching them exit one by one. Then they put the man hole cover on. I wait for a few moments, hoping they will leave.

It is one of the other executives. He climbs back down in the man hole. "I know you're in here. We asked Hazel who you were. She didn't know you."

But the whole time he is talking, I am standing in front of the ladder way of the other man hole. He doesn't know I am there. But yet he keeps on talking while I am bending away on the bottom bar that has broken away from having something heavy fall on it.

He is walking toward me. The little girl never utters a word. "Oh, there you are."

"Yeah, here I am."

I don't know how many times I hit him. I hit him so many times, so fast, until I hear her grunt. I throw the bar down beside him and wait for the man hole to open again. When it doesn't, I go up the one that had the broken bar on the bottom.

"Look honey, it's gonna be okay. I'm gonna take you to the sheriff's station. Then we'll get you back to your mom and your dad."

I push on the heavy iron lid. It is a little heavier than I can handle with one arm. I have my back against the man hole while I hold her with the other arm. As soon as I am able to lift it up, I look down the alley way.

I lay the little girl down beside the man hole when I get her up. It isn't easy, and then I slide the man hole back into its place as I get out. I reach down to pick the little girl up. When I stand up and turn around, there she is, Nina.

She says, "Come with me if you want to live."

We walk for several blocks. I carry the little girl 'til my arms are about to fall off. Finally, we make it to a parking lot. It is a high rise building. It is about the third floor up when we enter into an apartment.

"What a night, huh?" I say.

"Okay, buster, let's hear it. Why do you keep calling me Nina?" she says.

"Why do you keep answering to her name? I killed her."

"*You* killed her?"

"I'm gonna kill you, too. You're all gonna die."

"Nina was my sister. We were twins," she says.

Well, that explains a lot.

"I'm C.I.A," she says.

"You're what?"

"I work for the law enforcement. Do you understand that?

You're in the middle of an investigation."

"I'm taking the little girl to the police station."

"She'll be dead before the morning," she says to me.

"I know the sheriff," I tell her.

"That sheriff can't protect her. Nobody can. That new sheriff couldn't... well," she says as he walked backward and forward.

"Show me your badge," I question her.

"It's over there in my purse. I'll get it," she says..

"You stand right there. I'll get it," I tell her.

As soon as I open her purse, it's a revolver. A .38. I hate it.

"Keep digging," she says after she sees me pull the gun out and glare at her.

That's when I find her badge and her credentials. Hazel and her last name. "But you were fixing to kill the girl."

"I knew he wouldn't do it," she says. "I had him scared to death. I spent all day with him, telling him horrifying stories of how it haunted me."

"But how did you get in without christening, the empowerment?"

She puts her hands together and says, "Undercover work."

"Not the D.A."

"I'm afraid so."

But I can only think, "It runs in the family."

"Really?" I ask her.

"I had to be convincing," she says.

"I don't want to know the details."

"Relax, nothing happened."

"Why are you telling me this?" I ask.

"Because I see the look in your eye."

"What look?"

"You care," she says.

"I stopped caring a long time ago," I say. "While you're playing your little charades, children are dying."

"You won't stop that," she says. "It's too big."

"This empowerment, it ain't real. You know that, right?"

"Oh yes, I know it, but there's big money in it."

"What do you mean?"

"These college students, they're the elite of their kind. They're gonna make millions in their life time, just like you would have had you been christened. They're untouchable. But when I heard of the death of my sister, yeah, I would've slept with him. I would've slept with anybody. Some do gooder like yourself comes along—"

"Your sister wasn't a good person," I interrupt her.

"We were just alike."

"No, I don't believe you."

She walks over and picks up her gun from where I sat it down. I get kinda nervous, not for my sake. It's the little girl. She is asleep, in shock of what just happened and the witness of her parents being murdered. Hazel puts the gun by her side.

"What now?" I ask.

She swallows. I can see the lump in her throat go down. "I really loved my sister. I swore I'd kill her murderer, but the fact is she did me dirty. Real dirty, and I'm not too sure she didn't kill mom and dad. After falsifying the will and taking all the money."

"She wasn't murdered," I say. "Yes, it's true. I killed her. Just like I was gonna kill you."

"She just needed direction," she says.

"And I gave it to her." I stand in front of her. "What now? You gonna kill me?"

She looks down at the gun that she has in her hand. "Oh no! I've got the detailed report. I just didn't recognize you, and lucky for you, the D.A. didn't either. I've watched him kill three or four people."

"So, y'all aren't lovers?"

"He thinks we are. He woke up beside me a few times, thinking things happened."

"How does a man think that things happen when they don't?"

"Well, when you're passed out from being drugged... Okay, the fact is, me and my sister were nothing alike. She joined the sororities. I studied. She wanted to make money. I wanted to be a detective. I was all goody goody two shoes. She was reckless and careless. I know why you killed her. And I know why the sheriff let you go. A big long speech. No vigilante. Did he give you that? No, he let you go because he had a christening, too. They made him, but it wasn't long after that when he realized they had taken his little girl and done the same thing to her. And that deputy that took his place, he ain't no better."

"But why'd he let me go?"

"Guilt. He made it as far as Honolulu." Then she breaks down and cries as she finishes, "Before they skinned him alive."

"They what?!?!"

"You know what he died of? Hypothermia. See, you can't stay warm without your skin, no matter what you do. He literally froze to death. It was most agonizing death. I don't feel sorry for him," she says to me. "He wasn't a good person."

"I don't believe you. The old woman would have told me."

"She had to use him, and if you would've known it, things wouldn't have turned out the same. You wouldn't have said the same things or did the same things."

"I'm gonna kill 'em all. If you stand in my way, I'll kill you, too," I tell her.

She jerks my arm around with an angry voice. "You can't just go around killing people! And I'm not gonna stand by while you do it like the sheriff did. So help me, if you vigilante, you're going down with the rest of 'em."

"And you're gonna take 'em down?" I ask.

She shoves her gun back into her purse, along with her junk. "By yourself?" I ask. "While you watch innocent children slaughtered."

"Like I said, I took care of it. I called it in as soon as that D.A. said it was your turn."

"You called it in?"

"The fact is, had you not shown up, I would not have had to call it in. I had it all under control."

"What about the rest of these cults?"

"They're not a cult. Outside of these christenings, they believe in doing right. Now my sister, yeah, she was a little spiky if you ask me. Did she get to you?"

"She got to all of us," I say. "She made us think we were family."

She looks down. "She never made me feel that way."

"She made me feel incredible," I think to myself," as I say, "There was something about her. I don't know what it was."

"Oh, I know what it was," she says. "It's the way she made you feel. She believed it, you know? She said she believed it was necessary to be empowered. I had no idea what she was talking about at the time. I told her, 'Nina, you already have power.' She smiled and said, 'Not like I'm gonna have.'"

"But Nina's been dead for a long time."

"And yet her killer stands before me," she says.

But the fact was that I had loved Nina, in more ways than just one.

"You're such a coward," she said to me one time. "You're not free like me. I'm as free as a bird," she said. "I can fly anytime I want."

"Is that why you fly away, Nina?" I said to her. "Every time you feel you're gonna get close to somebody."

"Honey, I'm empowered. I make the feelings. I create 'em inside of me, so that I can give 'em to others. That's why I make you feel so good."

And she did. She was very convincing.

"I've just got one question. Why'd you answer me when I called you Nina the first time?" I ask Hazel, or whoever this is in front of me.

She walks up to me. "I was in shock when I heard you say that. I was ignoring you, not answering you."

It can't be. I think on it. Every little detail is exactly the spitting image of Nina. I have seen her from head to toe. I say, "It's amazing, Hazel."

"Yes?"

"Every little detail. How did you do it? There are no twins that perfect."

"That's what we are, perfect twins, night and day."

But could it be possible?

Could she have switched?

She is pulling on my heart.

Killer.

The first rule of the game.

No empathy.

No feelings.

If you can feel the good, you can feel the pain that goes with it.

I can't take it.

I remember standing over my girlfriend's body. I stood there for a while, thinking all kinds of things. But Nina was the one I was thinking about.

The BMW. The hotel. The men she had been with. The man that she had laid with.

The head master came to her one day. She was fresh in college, still a teenager. "A young girl like you could be empowered with millions of dollars."

"I'm already rich," she said. "I've got everything I want. I just need the paperwork from the college to prove my education."

"I'm gonna be a nurse," she said. "Or maybe a doctor."

But she ended up in stocks. Oh, she got millions just like he said. But the empowerment, a fourth of everybody's pay, from all their recruits.

"You're gonna make billions, and all you have to do is give us a fourth," he told her.

It was just another money making operation, and I am not convinced this isn't Nina. I didn't observe her so closely, watching her die. The water beat her cold body. But she didn't look the same. It was the look on her face. Something was different, but I couldn't bring myself to believe.

Could it have been Hazel that I shot?

Could she have switched places?

The little girl wakes up crying. "I want my mommy."

They killed her mother. They killed her father, too. And her little brother. Just like all the families, they would give 'em a chance. If you got invited, that was the end of your life as you knew it.

Hazel slides her hand into mine. "Come here. I wanna show you something."

I'm afraid of her. I am just about convinced it is Nina. It's the way she holds my hand when she pulls me over to her computer. It is a laptop, but it has fingerprint recognition. She slides her finger across it.

"My fingerprints," she says.

"You could have changed it. You could have switched it out for Hazel."

"You're convinced, aren't you?"

"I know it's you, Nina."

She slaps me across the face. "Quit calling me Nina. I'm Hazel," she says.

"No, you're not Hazel. Hazel laid dead in the shower. How

did you switch places? How did you do it?"

"Is there any way I can convince you otherwise?" she asks.

"No."

"How can you be so sure? You were in love with her, weren't you? You were in love with my sister."

I don't say anything, but now I am convinced it isn't Nina. She plays me off slow, getting every piece of information from me.

"That must have been the hardest thing in the world for you to do," she says.

"It would've been harder the second time around."

When I say that coldly, she shakes a little bit. I can tell it moves her. "So now you're convinced?"

I pick up the little girl. "I'm taking her to the police station."

"They'll kill you before you get there. They're everywhere, including the police station," she tells me.

"They don't know me."

"That sheriff knows you. Let me take care of it."

"I don't trust you. I just don't trust you. As far as I know, you could have somebody pick her up..."

She kneels down by the little girl. "Do you know where your momma and daddy are?" she asks her.

"They're dead. They're dead, Nina. They killed 'em."

"Why did you call me Nina?"

"All of 'em called you Nina, until he came."

"My name is Hazel, not Nina."

But I was there. I heard 'em call her Nina. I'm not the only one confused. That's if I'm confused at all. But I know it's Nina,

116

and so does the little girl.

"Do you know who killed them?" she asks the girl.

"They were in black, and one had a necklace on that was big. But the man's voice I heard sounded like the man that came over to my dad's house all the time."

"Would you know him if you saw him again?"

She shakes her head yes. "He's the one that stabbed my dad."

"She see all that?" I ask Hazel.

"Yes, I was there. They had me in a bad predicament."

"What are y'all waiting on? How many people's gotta die?" I get mad. "Y'all just watch people die and do nothing about it. How big does the case gotta be before it falls apart?"

"We were after the big dog," she says.

"Yeah, well who is that?"

"It is the Vivid Corporation," she says. "That's where I work at, undercover, of course."

The dean of the college works there, too. In fact, he owns it.

"So how long are you gonna sit back and watch people die before you do something?"

"I take orders. I do what I'm told. It took five years to get in this deep."

"I'm tired of talking. It's time for action."

She says, "So help me, if you get involved in this, I won't be able to protect you. You'll go down with the rest of 'em. A cold blooded killer."

"That's what I am," I say.

"You're beginning to believe it."

"I've always believed it. From the first time your sister told me about the empowerment, I knew exactly what she was talking about. Anybody able to take a life, the fear of God leaves 'em. And without hope, a man is empty."

I had hoped that I could save my daughter, but that hope is long gone.

"So that's it then? You're dead to the world, and to everybody in it."

"I got a new scenario for you. I'm gonna kill 'em all, and if you stand in my way, I'll kill you, too. And if this little girl gets hurt—"

"I'll take care of her. Don't you worry about it," she says.

"You better. Your life depends on it."

Her eyes open up wide. She realizes that the cold has set into my heart.

I walk out the door and slam it as I go out, wondering if I have done the right thing and also wondering why she is so excited.

The glare in her eyes.

She is fascinated with me.

But I only know too well why.

It is the empowerment.

It is deep inside of me, and she can see it.

But maybe it isn't her. But I've seen that look before, and there's something else I've seen before.

For forty-five minutes, I stared at Nina's naked body in the shower. But it was around her eye, and I could only see it when she closed her eyes all the way. And that wasn't very often. But when she closed her eyes, there was a small mole there. Nina didn't have a mole.

But it was when she gave me that look on the way out of the door. Almost like she could hug me. But when she shut her eyes, there was no mole. There was no birthmark at all. Just like the rest of her body. Smooth and silky. Ready to soothe her next victim into the bed, or into whatever she wanted him to do.

Or me, in that case. I try to shake it off, but my feelings are coming back.

Can it be Nina?

Chapter 12
Nina Lives

The afternoon newspaper. D.A. shot three times in the heart. Suffered after a gun shot to the belly.

I am paid a visit the next day. It's the latch on the door. As soon as he walks past the room door, I put a gun to his head. "Holster it."

"Alright now, take it easy. You and I are friends, right?"

"That depends on what you came here for."

"No vigilante, remember? We had a deal. There's been two more murders since the paper came out. The D.A., one was a policeman. You promised you wouldn't go back at it."

I take the gun back down from his temple. "It wasn't me. You got a new vigilante on your hands now. Besides, you got my gun."

"Yeah." He pulls it out. "I still got your gun, but what's that in your hand?"

"Oh, this, it's a mop handle. It broke off last night when I tried to get a rat out from under the refrigerator."

"There's been more kids missing." Then he begins to cry. "One of 'em is mine."

"Oh no!"

"Me and you are friends, right?"

"Yeah, Sheriff, we're friends."

"Please find him! Please, Mr. Hourson!"

I hadn't heard that in a long time. Mister.

"I'll do what I can."

I put my hand on his shoulder. After sitting down briefly, he stands up and walks out, but I look down on the coffee table. There it is. The .357.

I pick it up. No, there are no bullets in it, but I have plenty. Specially made bullets. I cut X's in the hollow points with a hack saw halfway through the bullet so when it hits, it will spear out into four pieces. I put those in the chamber.

From now on, it's gonna be one shot, one kill, one dead. I take my old holster and put it on. It's a shoulder strap. I throw the gun in there.

I go back to her apartment. She isn't there. Neither is the little girl.

"Oh God! I believed that little—"

And right before I get a curse word out or two, she walks right in the door with a bag of groceries in her hand and the little girl by the other hand.

"If you get seen with her—"

She says, "Don't worry. I've got it under control."

"What did you do to her face and her hair?"

"I made her look like my niece."

"Niece? Nina had a baby."

"No, my brother."

"So y'all have a brother?" I ask.

"Don't worry. He's up in New York. He has nothing to do with this."

I hardly believe her. I hardly believe anything she says, but she is really convincing.

After entering into the apartment, the little girl turns on the TV. Newsflash. District attorney caught in a gunfight. He was rushed to the hospital, only to die in intensive care. Eleven others were involved. Four were arrested. Two are at large. The others were found on the scene dead. If you've seen these people, contact your local law enforcement.

"Your twelve?" I ask.

"Yeah. I turned the case in, but they didn't even make it to the jail, the four that were arrested. I couldn't take a chance on 'em getting this girl again. I told you I'd take care of it."

"What about those at large?"

"They're not at large. They won't be found."

"You know that for sure?"

"I have a reliable source."

"Won't be found as in dead, 'cause if not, I'll make sure?"

"Okay, I'll spell it out for you. They're under concrete. They've become a part of the new foundation, and that's all I know. I wasn't there."

"Nina, don't lie to me."

"Blast you! Have you no respect for my dead sister?"

"Not one little bit," I say.

"Now you're the one that's lying. Did you love her that much?"

"Let's get one thing straight. I'm a killer."

But what am I saying?

I can't call it vigilante work.

I can't call it murder or homicide.

I do one thing.

I get rid of murderers.

But Nina's voice echoes in my mind. "Once you feel the power, darling, you'll be mine."

I don't know how, but I feel as if she is Nina. But then I remember why. It was in the kitchen. It was one of those American brand coffees, but really it was sweet potato.

"You got any real coffee?" I asked her.

She said, "I keep that old can. There's real coffee bean inside of it."

But when I opened the cabinet, there was another bag there.

"What? Hazelnut coffee?"

Well, I mixed it together. It was pretty decent.

It all seems absurd. C.I.A., F.B.I., an undercover agent. But how could I have killed the wrong woman?

There is one thing for certain. They were twins.

I get a hold of the sheriff. "I need you to look up something for me. The third woman I killed—"

"Now watch it now? I'm the sheriff now, not the deputy sheriff, and I don't let killers go. I put killers in jail, and that includes you. I ain't like the old sheriff. In case you don't know, bad things happened to him. I'm playing by the book. You know what I mean?"

"Yeah, I know what you mean."

The way he is talking could only mean there are deputies around. I write down some information. "Check out if Nina had a sister, and let me know if they were twins. I may have killed the wrong one."

When he reads that, his eyes get big. He shuts the door. "You mean to tell me this maniac could still be alive?"

Wheels begin to spin in his head. "That's what happened to my son," he says.

I say, "Hold on now, you don't know that for sure. Just run these numbers. If they come back with the correct equation, we're safe. But if it wasn't Nina laying in that shower..."

He has picked up a few habits from the old sheriff, rubbing his mouth, scratching the side of his head. He has gotten pretty good at it. But the information isn't easy to process. File errors everywhere. New entries. Old deletions.

He calls me over to his house. "Look, I wanna show you something. These are the files that belongs to Nina, and these files, they gone."

"What do you mean gone?"

"Gone! Deleted."

"What were they?"

"That's just it. I don't know. I was hoping you could tell me."

"It could mean nothing."

"I don't believe it's nothing, but I don't believe that's Nina that you're hanging around with."

"What?!?"

"Yeah, I've been keeping an eye on you, especially after the sheriff got his face whacked off."

"What do you mean whacked off?"

"All I got was a photo from the shoulders up, no skin. I couldn't even read the report after I saw the picture."

"I heard he was skinned alive," I tell him.

"See, there you go. Unwanted information."

"Sorry, Sheriff, you need to know what you're up against."

"You don't think I know what I'm up against? You were the roughest thing we run into in this state."

"But you know that ain't true, Sheriff."

"Well, I didn't know about all them killings. I didn't know nothing about no empowerment movement either."

"I gotta go. I gotta get back to Hazel."

"Hazel? Who's Hazel? Her twin sister's Demetria," he says.

"Do what?"

"Yeah, Demetria, or something like that. It wasn't Hazel by any means."

"You got that report?"

"No, but I can pull it back up on the computer."

After searching for several moments, he pulls it back up. There it is. Her full name. Hazel. That's the only part I am looking for.

"Now what were you saying about Demetria?"

He says, "I don't know. Maybe I was seeing things... No, it was something about a name change."

But what is she doing? Is she playing with the system, or is somebody higher up playing with it?"

"I need to tell you something else before you leave, you hear?" the sheriff says.

"Yeah, I hear."

"I've been on the system three times, and for three times, they've been different."

"Somebody in F.B.I. had to tap into this. Somebody high up. Maybe she's telling the truth. Maybe it's her boss getting her ready for her next assignment."

"Well, you can think what you want, but I ain't gonna believe nothing else. It's just a glitch in the system. That's all it is. Just a glitch in the system," the sheriff says.

"Well, thanks, Sheriff."

"Wait a minute. What about my young'en?"

"They recovered him."

"They who?"

"The F.B.I."

"And you felt the need to tell me this when?"

"When it was necessary."

"And when did you think it was necessary? That's my son!"

"Well, right now, that's the reason I told you. By the way, he's fine."

"She have anything to do with it?" he asks.

"Yes, she did."

"What about these other killings?"

"Somewhat."

"I just want you to know, Mr. Hourson. When the time comes, I'm gonna be the one standing over her body this time. But I hope for your sake, that that time don't have to come."

Now it's a year later. Yeah, I'm stupid. But I was already in love. But I haven't killed anybody in over a year, and I feel good about that. But my feelings are coming on strong. She never leaves my side. We kept the little girl. She's ten and a half, almost eleven. I can't help but to love both of 'em.

The old woman said, "If it ain't revenge, you'll recover." She was crying when she said that. "I regret I had to help you kill, but my heart's still tender for you. See, I had a son one time, and you got his same mannerisms."

And that sure wasn't a killer. He was obviously afraid of everything like I was. She had told me a story about how he was scared. That was my first story to tell her.

I was six years old, the beginning of my fears. It was a curve market one block up from where I lived. I had twenty-five cents in my hand. I pretty much walked anywhere I wanted. My momma worked days. My dad, I didn't know about a dad then. But it was a pack of Winchesters.

"A pack of Winchesters please."

"Well, that'll be fifty cents, young man. You getting these for your momma?"

"Yeah," I said, lying, of course.

I was pretty fearless up to this point. I knew the man at the register, and he knew me.

"What can I get for twenty-five cents?"

He said, "Nothing that you can smoke, I'm afraid. You can get you a soda pop and a candy bar, though."

127

"Really?"

"Yeah, go back there and grab you one, anything you want."

Now that was exciting. I grabbed a candy bar and opened it up. I went back to the freezer, slid the door open, and reached down. Coca-cola. I reached over on the side of the freezer, popped the top on that thing, and boy, them suds came out. I drank it straight down. My eyes were watering.

Now I was feeling really good inside. That's when I heard the bell to the door ring. A great big ol' gun. Two of 'em. One had a pistol, and one had a shot gun.

"Where you keep the cash at?"

"Right here in the register like everybody else."

He poked him with the gun, the shotgun. "I won't ask you again. Where's the safe?"

"There ain't no safe. I don't make but a little money."

He hit him in the head with the butt end. His eyes rolled back into his head, and he fell behind the counter.

"Get back there and wake him up!"

After he got back there, he said, "Uh, there ain't no waking him up." He let him fall back to the floor. "He's dead."

"That's murder, you know?"

He took the shot gun and shot him. Now I was at the end of one of the racks. I just slid into that back room, and I skivvied over into the corner. He was ransacking the whole store. He never did find what he was looking for, but when he came in that room, right where I was at, he jerked stuff around, banged stuff around. But there was a box in front of me, and it was the only thing hiding me.

He reached over and picked the box up, and before he looked down, I was shaking so bad I used the bathroom on myself and held my breath 'til I almost passed out. That's when I heard a bell ring again, and so did he. It was the front door.

A customer came in. He went out the door. I heard the gun go off again, and I jumped so bad I hit my head on the desk up above me.

She shook her head the whole time I told her. "I've been afraid of everything ever since then."

"Well that explains it," she said. "Why that little blonde haired hussy wants you in so bad. She's trying to make a man out of you."

I said, "Killer. She tried to make a killer out of me."

"I want her dead," I told her. "More than I wanna live."

But when I heard about the disappearance of another kid, that's when my heart went cold. I asked her to help me.

She said, "I'll have to go back to some old hook ups. He's an old judge now, but back then, he was a cocky young lawyener." She couldn't say it right.

"You mean lawyer?" I asked, smiling real big.

She said, "Yeah, you know what I mean. I ain't got no teeth, you know?"

It wasn't too long after that, though, that she did have teeth, and nice clothes. When the old judge found out how she had been living, he wouldn't hear of it.

She said, "I used to be a looker at one time."

I said, "A hooker?" laughing, of course.

She said, "No, a looker. Good looking."

"Well, I thought you surely meant hooker because you're still a good looker."

"Oh, you're just joshin'."

"Well, you look alright. That's all I can say." She did look a lot better after she got her teeth.

She said she was gonna go through with it. She was gonna help me. After talking to that judge, she felt obligated. He had told her, "The D.A. is out of control."

She didn't go into any details about it. She said, "But I'll take care of it."

The judge said he was untouchable. "He's getting protection from high up," the judge said, "and that detective ain't helping matters. Whatever you got planned, you better do it quick. They're trying to bar me off the bench. But with the new election coming up, I'm sure to be outta here anyway. But I'll do whatever I can to help you."

———————————

"You still call me by her name when we're intimate," Hazel tells me.

"I do not. I would never do that."

But I don't mind spending every minute with her. She's perfect. It was only three weeks after we had been together.

"I quit my job," she said. "I never had to work anyway. I was thinking along the lines of vacation. I wanna live on a mountain close to the sea. Europe maybe?"

"Let me guess, you wanna play family for a while. Is that what you're saying?"

"Oh, we're family, alright, and if we're gonna raise this girl, we're gonna have to make it right with her."

I believed everything she said.

I wanted to believe everything she said.

She was great. She was a great mom.

The girl is about to turn fourteen. She is quite beautiful. She wears the fanciest dresses. It's Iceland. With the glassed in porches, you can hardly recognize the cold hard winters that last so long.

But the rule is, once in, no way out.

There's a big duck or a goose in the yard. She goes out the door. I watch plainly through the glass. If the old woman would have been alive, the sight of this would have surely killed her. I watch the girl's hair fly up off the side of her head as her head looks like a bat hit it sideways as she sinks slowly to the ground like a board falling over as the wind blows the rest of her hair. I can hardly believe my eyes. It looks like two puffs of smoke hit the glass right in front of me, bullet proof glass. It is over an inch thick.

Before I know it, Hazel has tackled me. I am still in shock from what I saw. The front porch door busts into flames. The door busts into the house and busts the house door down. The percussion knocks both of us six to eight feet away from where we were at before. I fly up against the table and hit my head. I am unconscious.

I wake up throwing up from a concussion. I can't even pick

my head up. I remember bits and pieces. One laid dead in the yard, two on the porch. I couldn't see in the house. There were all kinds of patrol cars, inspectors I believe.

My eyes roll back in my head again as I pass back out. Four days, three nights later, I wake up. I don't know where I'm at, and the best part is I don't care. I have no remembrance of the little girl at all, but when she walks in the door and grabs my hand, I would know her anywhere.

Nina.

"Oh my God, you're alive!"

She begins to cry. "I don't know how to break this to you, but I'm Hazel, Nina's sister."

"Nina, I'd know you anywhere."

"He has suffered mild amnesia," the doctor tells her.

"When will he get his memory back?"

"I'm afraid never, judging by the wound to his head. Several centimeters of his brain matter were damaged. I'm afraid it will only get worse from here."

"You mean...?"

"Yes, I'm afraid so. There's nothing we can do for him."

"Doc., I'm right here, you know, right? You're talking as if I'm dead."

He looks at me, and then he looks back at Hazel, at least that's what she says her name is, and I think it is terribly rude when he just walks out of the room and never even consults me at all.

"Why ain't I afraid?" I think.

I get up off the bed. I am dizzy at first, but I am more angry.

"Where are you going?" Nina asks, I mean Hazel.

I open the door. "Hey mister! I'm talking to you!"

He turns around and looks at me. "Respect!" I yell at him.

"I apologize, Mr. Hourson."

"I'm sure glad you are because I was about to mop the floor up with your head."

His eyes get really big.

"I don't think your bedside manners are up to par, and I want a second opinion," I tell him.

"I am the second opinion, but the head doctor's on staff if you want to talk with him. He said there was something that could be done, but it was quite costly. Two hundred and fifty thousand dollars."

That's when I collapse to the floor. I wake up two and a half weeks later in intensive care again. Here she comes again. This time, my head is all bandaged up. I look at her. A million things go through my mind.

She grabs my hand and begins to cry. "Do you remember anything?"

"She's dead."

She nods her head yes and begins to cry. Sobbing, she says, "Do you remember anything else?"

"No, I'm kinda confused."

"Do you remember us?"

"Yeah, I remember us, in two different worlds. When can I get out of here?"

"As soon as they take the bandages off of your head."

Six weeks later, she says, "I re-enlisted, so to speak."

But I have no idea what she is talking about. They have tested my memory, but now that I am out of the hospital, I realize some of the things that I should remember, I don't remember. I don't remember killing Nina, and I don't remember her having a sister.

But I do remember being in love with her, but Nina doesn't cry, and she doesn't laugh for joy for others, only for herself. Nina doesn't grab my hand. Nina grabs anything but my hand.

Tears? They are like the fading sun in the afternoon, behind the mountains and gone, long gone. But when I turned off that water, that wasn't shower water that was going down her cheeks. That was the only time Nina cried, and I didn't even have the pleasure of the remembrance of it.

Or of killing anybody. I was a nice ol' guy again.

"Would you kill for me?" I ask her.

"Silly, surely you remember the last explosion. Your head injury."

"Yeah, I remember."

I get real serious. "Only somebody military trained—"

And before I can get my words out, she says, "C.I.A. Remember? I am military trained."

She has all the bases covered. Either she is the twin sister, or I am too in love to care. When the empathy of your memories are gone, so are the solitudes and convictions. And with no solitary convictions to base my memories on, like my daughter, and Nina raving on for Sara to kill her, I am left destitute and dependent on her for every little thing. And she knows it.

The fear is back. She looks at me like a poor puppy dog and begins to make passionate love to me. She begins to act exotic and out of control after she ties my hands up to the bed post. She goes at it full blast with her passion. I look up at the ribbons that are tied around my wrists. I try to pull 'em loose, but they cut into my wrists. She takes more ribbon.

I try to kick it away. It is no use. She lassos one foot and ties it down at the foot of the bed along with the other one and has her pleasure for forty-five minutes while she smiles at me the whole time.

I'm in horror. The pain of pleasure is exasperating. I think of my wife. My daughter. And I think of that little girl. It all starts coming back to me.

"I'll kill you this time," I think.

She licks me on my neck, and my ear, and across my eyes. "Ooh, I could just eat you. You're so frigid, fresh."

She is insane.

"I'm ready to come out now," she says, "'cause now I truly love you."

That's when she pulls her hands around, the same dagger that killed my daughter. She puts it at my throat and pulls it down very, very slowly.

"Nina, don't."

"She was my best friend, you know. She begged you, and then she begged you to kill her," she says.

Everything clears up then. Still in the middle of intimacy, she reaches down and kisses me on the lips.

"Nina, don't kill me."

"We're all past that now. I have to kill you. You've taken my powers away, and with this new found fear of yours, I have to kill you slowly."

"You're wrong about me. I would kill you right now."

She cuts my left hand loose. "You'll have one chance."

She puts the dagger in my hand, and at the bottom of her rib cage, between her breast, she aims the dagger and pushes it in a little bit with my hand inside of hers.

But I can't do it. She has mesmerized me or something. I can't explain it.

She shakes her head slowly. I let her tie me back up. She kisses me again, still in the middle of intimacy. She goes down in the middle of my chest at the bottom of my rib cage and begins to push the dagger in very, very slowly.

The pain is so deep to start with, I barely feel it at first. A big smile comes on my face, and a frown comes on hers and wipes her smile away.

"I love you, Nina," I say as I look deep into her eyes. "I love you."

She looks even deeper into my eyes. "I love you, too."

She pushes the dagger a little deeper. The pain gets a little worse. I can't close my eyes. I take in my last breath when she pushes it just a little deeper. I can't suck in another breath of air.

"Please, Nina."

She pushes it just a little farther as genuine tears fall from her eyes. She is a killer. Every move I made, she was there.

The D.A. was the head of all of it. "The ultimate power, Nina, it isn't to be able to kill one that you're close to, but to turn that which is close from fearful to its unfearful heights and then crash it into fear once again."

She smiled at him, and just like the other eleven, she pulled

136

out a gun. "Down on your knees."

"You can't be serious, Nina. I'm the head master. My family started this organization, my Dad and his dad before him."

She stepped behind him. "I won't ask again."

She put her hand in front of the barrel just above it to keep the splatter from hitting her and lifted it up just a little as he knelt down on the ground.

"Put your hands behind your back."

"No! I won't do it!"

"Fine then."

She pulled the trigger. Her hand kept the blood from hitting her face, and each one, she murdered one after another one. The last one she shot the same way.

"I never did much like killing kids," she said.

Chapter 14
The Loop

But it was several years ago. The phone rang. "Demetria?"

"Yes, who is this?"

"It's me, your sister."

"I don't have a sister."

"It's me. Nina."

"Nina. What do you want?"

"I need to see you. I feel terrible for what I've done."

"You should feel bad. You stole my inheritance."

"That's why I wanna see you."

"Yeah, I'm listening."

"I'm gonna give you your part."

"Yeah, what's the catch? How come I don't believe you, Nina?"

"I'll explain it all to you. Fly here today. I've already set up the tickets on the net."

She hung up the phone. "Well, that's good news," she said.

She boarded a plane, just like Nina said to do.

"You'll have to get a cab from the airport to the apartment," she said. "No matter you do, make sure you're here on time. I wouldn't wanna miss our grand gathering."

"No tricks, Nina. You hear me? Not like last time. You cleaning out Papa's safe like you did."

"I was saving it for you," she said. "I heard what Papa had planned. We weren't gonna get any inheritance."

"Nina, that's not true! He left us everything. I don't know where you got that information, but it's far from the truth."

"It doesn't matter now. What's done is done. If you want your part, come and get it."

She said, "I've got a special treat for you, just like old times. Hazelnut coffee."

She hung up the phone.

The cab let her off at the apartment, but when she got there, there was a note on the door. "Take a hot shower, get ready to go. We're going out to eat. We're gonna celebrate. Take your time in the shower. I'll be back in forty-five minutes."

Nina had seen me following her closely. I didn't know it at the time, but I had lost her in the midst of following her. That's when I was in trouble. She would know me anywhere. I went back to her apartment after following her there several times. But this time I saw her go into her apartment building. This was days after she had followed me back to my house, my apartment, and even the other cottage, and even out to the island. I had no idea I was being tailed. Had I only had been as transparent as she was, but when I saw her go into the building the day I shot her, that's obviously where she pulled the switch.

139

But how did she know I was gonna kill her then?

Only a few minutes before she entered in, her look alike showed up. Nina went in the front of the building and disappeared out the back. I went up to the apartment, still not knowing that I had been discovered. The new girl knew nothing about me and obviously knew nothing about Nina, if it was her sister at all.

But now I know, her sister laid dead in that shower, and not Nina. I think on these things as I fade out, as darkness fills my eyes and the pain begins to fade away. But all I can see is her eyes looking at me. I am glad it is her, and I am glad it is finished once and for all.

After she kills me, how she does it, nobody knows. Where she disappears to, no one ever sees her again. Maybe an estate. A banker's wife. A king's queen.

I'm not there to stop her. Oh yeah, the empowerment organization, she got it in her head that the ultimate empowerment was to engulf its empowerities, which meant anybody and everybody that had empowerment would be absorbed by her wicked imagination of power hunger.

It is only ten years after she murdered me, in the coldest, cruelest way. It is in a dark, cold, and drafty cellar. Four beams in the middle, eight feet apart. A table with straps on it. A beautiful woman lays there, unclothed.

She wakes up. A hooded man is sitting on her stomach. She screams out when he puts a dagger in between her breasts, pulls it down beneath her rib cage, and begins to tenderly talk to her with a loving voice as he pushes it in slowly, saying, "I love you,

Nina."

That's when she remembers. She heard me come into her apartment and quickly went into the bathroom. I heard the shower going. She hid in the closet door as I walked into the bathroom. She very carefully and slowly opened the door just a little bit and watched me stand in front of the shower.

She jumped a little bit as the gun went off. When she opened her eyes, she could see the glass falling down on her sister's legs. A big smile came on her face. She stood there thinking to herself as she watched me stand over her dying sister, how amazing I was to her.

"This is the ultimate power," she thought to herself. It was me. She slowly pulled the closet door tightly closed and sat back against the closet wall in the dark, listening to every word I spoke.

I didn't even realize at the time what I was saying, how I loved her. I thought I was cold, but as she listened to each word, I became her obsession.

"But for now, I must remain dead," she thought.

After I walked out of the apartment, she walked out, too. As I went out the front, she went out the back. She stood there watching me at the end of the alley cross over at the end where I had came out the front and disappeared across the street as I went behind another building.

"I love you, Nina," he says to her with a tender voice. "I genuinely love you."

She shakes her head with her eyes wide open in terror. "No! No!"

As he pushes it deeper, ever more slowly, he repeats the words, "I love you, Nina."

"No, this can't be happening!" she thinks to herself as in her memory, she opened the closet door and walked out past her naked dead sister.

"I missed you the last time, but I didn't miss you this time," she said to her, thinking how gullible her sister was, how she had tried to kill her as Nina had killed her mother and father.

When she went up to the bedroom and found the will, her name wasn't on it. They were leaving everything to Demetria. That's when she had poisoned their meal, but Demetria didn't eat of it. That's the reason she was still alive. She had left to go to Paris, and a month later when she came back, her parents were buried. Nina had taken the will and changed it over.

That's how she ended up here.

Laying her life down for the empowerment.

Trying to scream.

Looking deep into her seducer's eyes as he pushes the dagger in a little farther, remembering how she had convinced him with her seductions and her lies.

"I can make you invincible," she had said.

Her next victim.

Her would be lover.

He fell for her lies and her seducing ways, only to be intrigued as he pushed the dagger in a little farther and said again, "I love you, Nina."

Chapter 15
Almost Family

But the truth be known, the sheriff knew me my whole life. Something to do with my mom before she died. I don't know, maybe a distant cousin or something. My dad would have probably told me had he not died soon after. All of my family died at a very young age.

But the sheriff was mad. "How could you do this?!? You're afraid of everything!"

But this was only after the deputy went out the door and shut it, and he had done it quite regularly throughout the day. He finally couldn't take it anymore.

"Sheriff, why is it every time I go out that door, I hear you yellin' and carrying on, but when I come back in here, you're calm and cool?" the deputy sheriff said.

The sheriff told him, "I don't know. I let my anger get the best of me. Ain't you glad you wasn't in here?"

But he mumbled as he went out the door, "I don't know. I probably wanna be in here with all the excitement. God only knows how boring it is out here. This dead beat town, nothing, nothing ever exciting. Even the killers turn themselves in."

But each time he grilled me.

"You know the D.A. wants murder charges. Murder in the first degree. You knew these people."

He remembered seeing some of us together, and he began to cry. "Y'all were good together?"

"You been away a long time, Sheriff. New York softened you while you were gone."

"Well, that was years ago."

"A lot's happened since then."

"But where have you been all this time?" he asked.

"I'll explain it all to you. You're just gonna have to be patient with me. If you don't like the way it's turning out, I'll sign your murder charges. The fact is, they can't put me to death for killing somebody, but murder, now that's a different story. Life and one day, that ain't what they want."

"They? They who?"

"The empowerment. It's the t double e. The Elite Empowerment."

"I heard something about that," he said, "but that was a long time ago."

"Well, the organization has grown since then. The twelve are not the only ones I've killed."

The fact is, I was empowered. I was obsessed with the feeling that I felt. I was a hero, not a murderer. I had saved many children and killed many of their leaders, only to have another rise up in its place. They believed it. They were convinced. Those

144

that started the committee never killed anybody, just the college kids that took their places as they got older.

Jean Aldo, the head of the organization throughout the entire committee and committees. The t double e was everywhere, and they were convinced. It was Nina, her bewitching powers to convince someone that they could be invincible by not only taking their life but everything they trusted in. You. The organization died out within a few years after my death. The head of the organization died out before I could get to him.

But this is an old man. Nina had met him years ago.

"This one's a tricky one. You're gonna take care of me, right?"

"What do you mean, Nina?"

"If he kills me, I want him to die the exact same way, but in an alley. Not some place prominent, but where everyone can see that Nina had been here, even after her death."

The old man stands on top of him, the one that killed Nina. He gives him a shot. It paralyzes his body, but he can feel and sense everything. He just can't move. The old man drags his body into the alley way, takes off his shirt, and begins to tell him, "I love you. It's me, Nina," in the old man's voice as he pushes the dagger into his chest the same way the one he is killing had done Nina not too long ago.

The old man gets up and laughs. "Nina was a special one. She would have wanted you to think that it was her killing you, and you being the head of the organization now and having only one kill but with Nina under your belt you got one hundred and one kills, making you the head of the organization. No, make it one hundred and two for Nina, counting you."

He slings the dagger over into the man hole. It is found years later and put into a museum as an ancient relic, and on the blade, it reads, "You'll be doomed for power if you place me in your hand. Only if you push me slowly as I guide your hand."

But on the other side, it says, "Don't be a fool by what you read. Once you take me, you must bleed."

And it is true about the old dagger. Every one that took it in their hand committed a murder, and every one ended up murdered the same way, included the head master of the museum. But I didn't have a dagger. Bewitched by some kinda source. Or some kinda chemical. But I had never touched the old dagger. What did it have against me?

I used a gun. But all I could think when I was laying there, when I was dying... I could no longer feel the pain. But at least it wasn't messy like I had left so many dead.

Those that got to the sheriff, they were the messiest. I carried two .357's. One I called Merciful, full metal jacket. The other I called Merciless. It stayed in my right hand.

There were three of them. They killed the sheriff, mutilated his body. I really liked him. But it was a rundown motel. A line of seven motels in a row. The cheapest you could get by any means. They were loud and obnoxious, bragging about their kills.

I was very good at what I did. I cut the sheet rock in the room next door after renting it. Four feet wide all the way to the top of the ceiling and down. I took the sheet down. I cut a big x on the back from corner to corner on the next piece after removing the little bit of insulation that was there.

Merciless in the right hand. Merciful in the left. I entered into the room by smashing through the x. I shook the dust out of my hair as quickly as I got in the room. One was at a desk at a chair, no gun. He was facing me. Some kinda swimming trunks on, I think. The other one had just come out of the bathroom with a robe on, and their partner sat there on the phone.

He had just hung it up when Merciless got him in the knee cap. You could see the bed behind where his knee used to be. His leg dangled. His eyes rolled in the back of his head, and he screamed out in pain as he grabbed the upper part of his leg. But before he could do anything, I had done the same thing to the other two.

The one at the desk rolled out into the floor screaming, "Oh God! Oh God!"

The other one fell toward the bathroom. Only his head made it to the bathroom when he began to scream, "Please, don't kill me! Please! I beg you!"

I stood there a moment and walked forward three steps. He released his knee, opened the drawer there beside the bed, and went for his gun. Another shot in his elbow. It blew his lower arm completely off. With nothing but a one inch piece of skin attached to it.

They were all three bleeding out. He scrunched down into the floor beside the bed where I couldn't see him, where he thought I couldn't shoot him anymore, and with the other hand reached under the bed and grabbed a pump shot gun with double aught.

I saw the barrel, took old Merciful, and shot through the bed three times toward his head. The gun dropped and then went off and shot the other guy beside the desk right in the head. "That wasn't nice," I said. "Matter of fact that wasn't nice at all." It scattered what was left of his face on the desk and the wall.

I wanted him to suffer. He was the one with the knives, the one that had cut the face of the sheriff up, mutilating his face while he begged him to stop while he ripped his skin off.

But there was still one left. But when I looked back toward the bathroom, his head was where I couldn't see it, but his body was in plain view. At least a half a gallon of blood had leaked out of his leg in the short process, and his stomach and ribs didn't move. I was quite sure he was dead. "Oh what the heck." I shot him in the chest anyway, then I shot him again.

Then I loaded the bullets up again with the real thing, X cutters, and I began to shoot 'em the more. I had never seen so much red in all my life, and it quickly darkened as I quickly over the next three hours cleaned up the sheet rock mess, put a new piece of sheet rock up, floated it, sanded it, painted it, walked out the door, locked it, and went next door, put the insulation back in the wall, put sheet rock back up, and did the same thing, and went to sleep. By morning, the paint was dry on both sides of the wall with more insulation than it had to start with. It needed it.

Killer.

Yeah, I was a killer.

And if I was empowered by anything, it was greed.

The greed for Nina's love.

I had killed her so many times in my mind that my heart was far from it.

Aching for my daughter, and wondering how she would have turned out had I not been the scared little boy that she called daddy.

At least, I didn't die a coward. I was a hero, and nobody knew it.

Chapter 16
'Til Death Does Its Part

The elderly do gooder was wonderful, at least that's what they thought, but it was only when I was stalking her that I found out the truth. It was so bad I wouldn't even speak it, even now, what she had been doing with the children. My daughter was the only one, and myself, ever thrown into the ravine. Most of the other bodies never showed up, thanks to her.

But she was an old woman. But she had been doing it a long time. I shook with anger. Sweat poured off of me. Unaware that I was in her office or unaware I was in her bedroom or maybe it was on the porch. No matter where she was at, I was there, stalking her every move.

She was just an old woman, sickened in her ways. But I couldn't understand it for the life of me. She did so much good. She worked in the soup line, doing good for the community, and smiled at every one, looking 'em eye to eye as if she was the most trustworthy person.

I could have killed her anywhere. But I had to let her know at least that it was me that killed her, and then I would end her suffering once and for all. But once I had rang that doorbell, there was no turning back when she opened that door. The surprise on her face and the look that she gave me, it was almost as if she wanted to say she was sorry.

After introducing the head of the organization, she told me her name. "I volunteer down at the soup line, and I work at the bakery, and I also own a restaurant. After five every night, I give free food away to those that can't afford it. Why don't you and your daughter come on down?"

She patted me on my shoulder as she walked by me. Yeah, we ate there, almost every night, for free. Why wouldn't I? It was great food, and she was great people when she was there. But the soup line, it wasn't no worse food than what she had in her restaurant. It just didn't add up. There was no money coming in, but there was plenty of money going out.

"We take care of our own, young man. You'll soon find that out," she said.

"She's just an old woman," I thought. "What does she know? She ain't making no money, and she ain't making no sense."

But everybody liked her. But something was wrong. Something made me suspicious, and I don't know what it was. The money. Too nice. Nobody's that nice to everybody. I know I wasn't.

I was grumpy when I woke up.

If you were around, look out.

I was grumpy before I went to bed, so if you were around, look out.

I was even grumpy writing this, knowing that I am dead,

because I know if you're reading it, then the score was settled. It's over with, and that's just how it is.

I had a gift.

It was a rare gift.

But I had glimpses of the future.

A glimpse of myself.

It was like a spider web in every direction. I could see the end of every decision that I would ever make, or wouldn't make. But one decision that I would change that I needed to change, none of this would have happened had I not been afraid from the start.

Afraid of women.

Afraid of friends.

I was even afraid of my daughter.

For my own selfish reasons.

The biggest reason was that if she died, I wouldn't be able to survive. I would go insane and die. I just knew it.

But Nina made me feel so good. She took it all away, the pain, the suffering that I had been going through. All at the same time, she added double. She had me wrapped around her finger so tight that I was glad the dagger never reached my hand until the day she killed me with it.

The old woman said she talked to the sheriff. But I had no idea it was this sheriff. It wasn't long before our disappearance when he came back from New York, so I had no idea it was the sheriff I had grown up with. But he wasn't a sheriff when I was a little boy, and before my daughter ever reached the age of ten, he had left to go to New York, his new career, which didn't pan out, and neither did his leaving at such a desperate time.

But there he came through the door for the first time. "I talked to the sheriff," she had said. "He's a stubborn one. He didn't believe a word I said, especially when I told him who you were."

I had kept the address at the apartment. The police questioned me about the murder. But my act was overwhelming. I curled my wrist and my fist up and pulled it up under my chin, and with a little slobber coming down out of the right lower half of my jaw, I slurred and stuttered.

"We're not gonna get nothing out of this guy," they said.

But I never did see the sheriff until the interrogation room. The first thing he said was, "I can't believe my eyes. I don't even believe it. I'm not gonna believe it. There ain't no way, no how."

I said, "Every bit of it's true, Sheriff."

"Half the police department wants you to hang. The other half wants you to suffer. Once you go down this road, there ain't no turning back."

"I'm guilty, Sheriff. That's all I can tell you. I killed 'em in cold blood."

As soon as the deputy left, he raved on about the paperwork. "It's not me charging you!" he screamed out. "The D.A.'s over this case. I answer directly to the detective in charge. I've got no choice, son. I've got to go by the book. This was first degree murder and nothing less."

He argued and screamed at me. How could I do it? I'm nothing but a cold blooded murderer. He yelled out until the deputy walked in.

I said, "I'm not a murderer." I said it over and over again. "I'm a killer. This I know. But murder, I'll never sign it. I'll never confess to that."

He grilled me hour after hour, thinking that I would have broke by then and confessed that it was all a lie. It took some convincing, but I never raised my voice one time. Until I yelled out in the middle of his arguing and raging and looking for the deputy to come back at any moment.

"Wait a minute!" I screamed. "This has gone far enough. You didn't even believe I was alive when the old woman came and told you about me. You laughed her to scorn. Yet, here I am."

"But you're so cold blooded," he said.

He spread the pictures out. It almost turned my stomach. It didn't look that bad when I was there. There was blood everywhere in the pictures. It didn't look like a killer had went through. It looked like a homicidal maniac had gone through with a hatchet.

He demanded that I have compassion, yelling at me, "Don't you feel anything?!?!"

But the truth be known, I didn't know if the deputy was in on it or not. Yes, the woman had saved my life, but now she had died, telling me, "The sheriff, I believe you can trust him, but I ain't too sure about that deputy."

But which deputy? And I wasn't too sure about her prejudice. So I over looked what she had said about the deputy, and my faith turned out good in him. And my faith really paid off when he saved my life. He knew exactly what to do to stop the blood when I was shot. I thought I had died then.

The sheriff said, "You owe him a great deal of thanks. The paramedics said if he wouldn't have been here, you wouldn't have made it." He never did tell me what all he did, and neither did the deputy.

My first kill, outside of the twelve, but still during the process of killing them. It was those that knew me, like when I went through the mall. It was the way they carried themselves, like they were invincible. A pride that was unstoppable. They looked as if they had a thirst that was unquenchable, devouring whatever they would and could.

I was on the top floor. It was a four story mall. The high priced slacks and shoes gave him away. That walk. Down a long hallway, he sensed me somehow. I don't know how. To everyone else, I was transparent. Out the exit door he went. To another brick hall way with a brick wall that led down a ramp to the first floor.

As soon as I opened the door, he turned around. "Why are you following me? Have you been empowered, my friend?"

He made an insignia with his hands. I didn't know what that was all about. Three shots in the chest. I put my gun up and walked back in the mall. I sat down at the ice cream parlor and ate ice cream, looking for another one.

You could tell right away, their costly apparel, their high standards of life, and they were nice to everyone. Not so much as one person passed by them that they didn't reach out and try to consume. It was worse than any plague.

But something was starting to move in me. She was obnoxiously happy. You could tell she was in her sixties, but she dressed and acted like she was forty. Too much makeup and too much plastic surgery. From her feet up to the top of her head. She was obnoxiously loud.

She was talking to a couple when I walked up to her. When she saw me, she knew who I was. "I've been empowered," I said.

She looked around quickly and shushed me down. "Shhhhh! You're to never talk of those things," she said with her little Italian voice, the way she rolled her r's, way more than she should have.

She grabbed my arm while she did that. I jerked away, walked away very abruptly, and pretended as if I had left the mall. I was very covert. She had seen us with the twelve, my daughter and I. But they had never formally introduced us, like the twelve were introduced into our lives. But here and there, we met new people, aboard yachts, trains, the scuba diver instructor. They were everywhere.

But I had a hey day. It went to my head.

———————————

"Nina!"

I had woke up crying one night, "You've got to stop, Nina!"

Only to look over at my girlfriend, my fiance'.

Nina walked into the room in a neglige. "Come with me," she said.

"Now!" she said.

I quickly got out of the bed. "You're gonna wake up—"

And before I could say another word, she put her hand over my lips and said to me with a stern voice, "She's a heavy sleeper, and it doesn't matter if she is or not, you're coming with me."

She grabbed my hand and pulled me toward the door. But I looked back in the dark for I was the last one out when I saw her hit the pillow with her fist. She had lied to me. She did care, and Nina didn't care about anything but getting her own way.

"I don't know why she lets you stay the night," I told Nina.

"You want me to tell you why? I own her. Just like I own you."

"Nina, what's that supposed to mean?" I asked her.

"You're going to find out one day, and it will be the biggest surprise of your life. When you realize it's me that you've been in love with all along."

And she was right. She did own Delie. She was a low one on the totem pole. Nina was next in line.

I was terrified at Nina's voice. I thought Mr. BMW was at the hotel with her, but they were just there to set up the whole plan. She had played them all, planning every little detail.

But the one thing she didn't expect was for me to come back from the dead. That was beyond her comprehension of power. Oh, she paid big for her little concert. Millions. Setting up every little thing that happened. She was a master at creating, only to destroy so that she could be empowered with the ultimate feeling of what I call the nothing that you will always have and never possess.

Across the country we went. It was a train ride. The conductor let us raise down a window at a certain part of the train and stick our hands and our heads out. We had the most wonderful time. My daughter sat on my knee. We went through a big town so fast that we were nothing but a blur as we went by. But sitting inside of that train, you would've never known it.

My daughter had started a game. "Come and play, Daddy."

She would get at one end of the car and run as fast as she could. "How fast was the train going, Daddy?"

"I don't know. A hundred and eighty-five."

She said, "How fast do you think I was going?"

"Oh, about two miles per hour."

She slapped down on my chest and said, "Oh, Daddy."

I said, "Okay, five miles per hour."

"That means I was going faster than the train. I was doing one hundred and ninety miles per hour. Five miles an hour faster than the hundred and eighty-five mile an hour train."

She had us all doing it. We took pictures. We all laughed. We had a great time.

One vacation after another one.

I was scared of everything. They called us scaredy cat and his fearless daughter. She was an average girl, but beside me she looked like a super hero. But she was no braver than any other girl her age. I embarrassed her a lot. I wished it could have been different.

We went everywhere in that train.

Another suspicion.

Three months out of the year, the twelve were constantly with me. We went on yachts, pleasure cruises. We even went on an airplane drop. The airplane goes straight down while you float in the center of it, free falling gravity. We took tons of pictures of everything.

It was the twelfth part of the initiation, your first kill, your intimacy with twelve others as you watched them be executed for the cause. Nina was on her last step. No more kills. No more killing. She would achieve the highest power called the twelfth position at the death of my daughter.

When it happened, she pulled that hoodie back and stroked her long beautiful hair as she held her head back, then she stretched her arms outward as if something were being poured on top of her. It was her twelfth kill. A big smile came over her face, then she raised her arms straight up in the air along with her head.

"You're a head master now," the head master told her.

She pushed him to the side. "I know what I am, and you, with your old ways, I'll have a new order," she said. "The greatest love, the greatest sacrifice."

He looked at her. "You'll never achieve it, Nina. You'll never be able to love like that."

"We'll just see about that," she said to him.

Not caring about me or my daughter.

They took the girl off the top of my daughter. She shook from head to toe. "Why don't I feel it? Nina, you said I would feel the power."

Nina looked at her as she walked away and grinned. "Well, I certainly do."

As soon as she found out I was alive, I didn't know it at first, but it was the movie I liked to watch with Nina and the girls and my other friends who I also killed.

"The heart's what I always shoot at," we watched on the movie. "Three bullets in the heart, there ain't no man coming back from that."

"The heart, is it?"

My favorite part, three days later... It's an old western, everybody's favorite actor. He was wearing a poncho and a Mexican hat.

"Watch this. Right in the heart," he tells his men.

But Mr. Eastwood had a steel armored plate underneath his poncho. The three shots to the heart didn't kill him, but the shot that he put in the man's head certainly killed his opponent.

Nina knew I loved that movie.

"Three shots to the heart," I said. "That's the only way to kill somebody, through the heart,especially in his earlier movies when he carried a .357."

I thought he was amazing. I watched the actor throughout the years. Sometimes I even imagined that I was him.

"Go ahead, punk, make my day." But I wouldn't dare say it out loud. I was too afraid someone would hear me.

But when Nina found out about the first victim, it was the three bullets in the heart that she caught wind of. She knew it would only be a matter of time before I found her, and she made sure of it. Just as she had expected, it was me, back from the dead.

———————

But it was after I drove by and thought I saw Nina in the hotel window. "You're late," she said. "I've been waiting for almost an hour."

"I had some business at the office. What's so important?"

"My plans, they better not fall through for your lack of support."

"It's not like that, Nina, and I don't like the way you're talking to me," Mr. BMW said.

"I'll talk to you any way I want."

He looked at her with a stern look. "Your obsession with power is far beyond realization. It's not real, you know."

She laughed. "But yet you kill again," she said and smiled at him.

"I only killed once."

"You've killed nine times, just like I've killed twelve. You killed every one of those kids just like it was nothing. What if one of your kids disappeared?"

"Wait a minute, Nina. That sounds like a threat."

"You do what I say. I'm the head master now," she said.

"Not of this group, you're not."

"You listen to me. You do what I say, and when the time comes, you better be on time."

She grabbed him by the face and kissed him. He pushed her away. "Don't try that girly stuff with me. It ain't gonna work."

"So you got everything you need you think?"

"If I could get out of this, I would've done it long ago."

"What's the matter? You afraid for your family? I would be."

But that was only too obvious. She had ran from a family hard and long, and starting a new one... A fast life has no rules. A family needs rules.

BMW got back in his car. I had a problem killing him, but I wanted him dead and I wanted it quick.

It was the phone call that he had made to his wife. "I just talked to Nina," he said. "...Yeah, she tried it again with her little seducing ways... Yeah, I went to the hotel again."

Lucky for him, I heard the conversation. It wasn't that I was jealous. It's just that there was no one like her.

Ever.

There will never be any one like her ever again.

She was training me. She knew I would pass by the hotel. She knew I would be enraged. But how did she know?

Yeah, Mr. BMW. "Come on, Mr. Hourson, you can't be afraid of everything. Diving is the simplest thing there is."

Liar! Too much nitrogen. I went belly up. Everything BMW talked me into, Mr. Fancy Executive.

"Man, you're my best friend. I wouldn't let nothing happen to you."

"Best friend? You have been a good friend. I appreciate it. But I'm keeping my feet on the ground from now on."

I was a stone cold killer. And I felt nothing for none of 'em. They set me up, got close to me, and the only thing I had as family was my daughter. She was more precious than my own life.

"Listen, son, this has been set up many times. It's a fail safe. If you do exactly what I say, we go all the way up to the president," the detective's mom said.

"I don't wanna be president, Mom."

"You can be whatever you wanna be. Just do what I say, you hear?"

"You manipulating everybody? Or just me?"

"Honey, I'm the one running the show."

He thought to himself, "Sounds like pride. I better be careful."

But when he heard of his mother's death, he wasn't moved at all. Matter of fact, he felt kinda glad. Her yelling. Her screaming. Her dictating. He had had enough, but yet, it was still his mother, if that's what he could call her.

But the more he thought about it, the more anger, the more emotion. But what about his empowerment? Was he really empowered? All this emotion, it was getting to him.

It was Friday afternoon. He knew the sheriff had heard an earful. "As soon as he brings him back to the cell," he thought to himself, "I'll kill him, the sheriff, and the deputy."

It was an old police shot gun. He had confiscated it years ago. But when he stepped into the cell room and didn't see the sheriff, the look on his face before he tried to shoot me was a look of unbelievable satisfaction. But it wasn't for his mom's sake. Like I had supposed.

She was arrogant, haughty, but only to him. To me, she

treated me like I was an angel child, always calling me son. "If my son was more like you..."

I said, "But I'm afraid of everything."

"But I see great potential in you," she said.

But I couldn't understand it. Her son wasn't introduced to me. But he was aware of everything.

Jealousy. Cruelness. Hatred. Bitterness. Strife. They hid it so well. And they were so rich and so popular. This was no way to get your kicks, unless you were like me.

A Killer.

Cold blooded, cold hearted.

Lifeless within.

But it was the detective's mom later on.

"I'm against it," he said. "You're not running the show. I am."

"You run the show?" she said. "Huh, that's a joke. You have never ran anything. Everything you do is a joke."

But he knew better than to talk back. She had things on him from way back, and he wasn't a killer. He was just a phony, pretending to be a killer, pretending to be empowered. Yeah, it was easy for him to watch.

Chapter 17
Can't Trust Anybody

I got a hold of some high dollar bullets. Six grand," the black market dealer said.

I don't need bullets," I told the man. "I need another three fifty seven."

"Thata be three grand," he said. "But you're gonna want these bullets. Electro magnetic pulsating bullets."

"Nah, just my regular full metal jacket the plastic tip ones," I said.

"They leave a clean hole," he said.

"Yeah, that's what they tell me. I also need the soft lead hollow points."

"These flatten out like a quarter," the black market dealer said, lying, of course.

But they didn't flatten out, as wide as a quarter for sure, but not quite as thick. Maybe the thickness of two quarters. But it was almost flat when it came out the other end, and everything from an inch inward coming out, it left a hole the size of a fist.

Looking in that way, you could plainly see through a person and their innards, but with three shots, those flattened out pieces of lead would hit that floor and skid right off of it back up into the body, slinging parts and blood upward everywhere. Just like I had seen in the pictures the sheriff showed me.

"Okay, demonstrate what they do, but I ain't payin' that much for 'em. I'm gonna tell you that right now. That's just crazy. I don't care what a bullet does."

"Let's just suppose you miss your target," the man said. "If this bullet goes in anywhere in a body, it is specially designed to do catastrophic damage."

"Okay, what does it do?"

"It's an electro-matic pulse. Let's just say somebody shoots you in the chest with one. What's your fillings made out of? Porcelain, metal, a mixture."

"I don't know. Why?"

"That metal in your teeth. The electro-matics in that bullet are ten times stronger than a car magnet at the junkyard. Your teeth aren't gonna move, but that magnet, it's gonna draw 'til it gets to those teeth. And the pulse, it's electro from the bullet to the teeth. It'll be electro shock every time it pulses, and every time it pulses, it puts out a hundred ton magnet, sucking it to whatever metal's in your body. For thirty long minutes, your body will jump all over the place, long after you're dead."

That was ideal for my next kill.

He had taken the dagger out of the blonde's hand and jousted me through with it. It was long and skinny, and it pierced straight through, crooked from one side over to the other side coming out the back. The gruesonility of the whole deal was I pondered over his body until the bullet ran out of its charge. His picture was the worst.

"This is where your three thousand dollars comes in at," the gun dealer said. "You better be fifty feet away because it's nuclear infused."

"What do you mean it's nuclear infused?"

"The little battery that's inside the bullet. Once it goes dead, it melts down and has a small explosion about twenty-five feet in circumference."

He said, "It ain't the explosion you gotta worry about. It's the radiation afterward."

"Well, that doesn't seem safe to me."

"Oh, they're safe until they explode inside that chamber. Once that bullet heats up, it activates it. Thirty minutes after that, you don't wanna be too close to it."

"I'll give you two grand for it."

"Ain't happening, man. Three grand. I've seen what these do to people. You absolutely wanna be the one shooting it and not the one getting shot with it."

"You give me two of 'em for one thousand. Or else, nothing else needs to be said, and I'll be on my way. I've got everything I came for."

"Okay man, if that's the way you wanna be, but these things are hot. I use 'em myself."

I said, "Let me see your gun."

He had a .45. He pulled out the clip and put the clip in my hand. I pulled the bullet off. "Yeah, they're special lookin' alright.

So you got 'em in .357?"

"I brought 'em specially for you, six of 'em."

"I'll give you fifteen hundred for all six of 'em. I'll pay you another fifteen hundred the next time I see you. If I make it back."

"Okay, man. Don't forget. Next month. Same time. Same place. Same as usual."

"Oh yeah, if I ain't here next month, go to my mailbox. Look in the very back of it. You'll know what to do."

"Okay, man, next month it is. Don't make me come looking for you."

But I only hoped that wasn't the case.

The young man, my next kill, came out of his bedroom, all sprawled back and cocky. He was clothed up to his waist without a shirt. He wasn't stocky, but he wasn't skinny either.

The twenty-eight year old that had thought he killed me the first time. I stepped out of the shadows and pulled my hoodie off of my head. He looked over at the gun. "Hey man, all I got is a couple of grand laying around." He raised up his hands with his palms toward the ground.

That's when I gave my guns names, Merciless and Merciful. But I only stuck one of those bullets in Merciless, and I stuck it in the last chamber. I wasn't even gonna use it on him. I had changed my mind. But I had forgotten I had spun the barrel before I stuck it in my holster.

The bullet went into his stomach. They were the worst shooting bullets I had ever bought in my life. "What a piece of crap!" I thought. It didn't even go through. It only went in about an inch.

"You shot me!" he yelled.

I came closer into the light.

"It can't be you! I killed you!"

His legs flopped out from under him. His head slammed to the floor, then his feet, and then it stopped and his body went limp. He went to breathing really fast. But all the sudden, like a fish flopping out of the water onto the ground, he began to flop again, and then it stopped as he began to bleed out of his nose and ears.

"What's happ—"

Before he could get the word out, it began again. He was banging his head so hard that it killed him, but the pulsating didn't stop. It wouldn't stop. Blood was coming out of every hole in his body. His feet had been beaten on the ground and his head so bad that it had slung blood everywhere. I couldn't believe my eyes. I had never seen so much blood in one place.

But there was another time.

There was another place.

There always was.

Just like the dealer said. Thirty minutes later. Only, it was only ten minutes later when I went out the door, and I got sprayed with a thin layer of misty blood.

"Thirty minutes," he said. I was only twenty-five feet away. I still remembered looking at the picture, nothing but brown glazed over blood, feeling nothing.

"Don't worry, buddy. I got your back," he had said. "I love you, man. We're all best friends, you know that right? We'll do anything for each other."

Now I really trusted this one.

"Daddy, I missed the bus."

"It's okay, Mr. Hourson. I'll take her. I'm gonna stop by the store and get some drinks, too."

He wasn't like the other one, showing special interest in my daughter. I trusted him in a different way.

"Yeah, I sure appreciate," I said. "I hate driving to the school."

He said, "I know how nervous you get. Why don't you tag along?"

"I'd like to stay here, if it's okay. If you don't mind, please."

"Sure, Mr. Hourson."

"Maybe I can get some food started while you're gone. Maybe sandwiches," I said, afraid of the burner, of course.

"I'll tell you what. Why don't I just stop and pick up some burgers?"

And that's just what he did.

"Yeah, that's my girl," he said as they took the blonde off the top of my daughter. "And this one's for free," he added as he turned around and looked straight into my eyes.

I didn't even know it at first. He pulled the gag off of my mouth and smiled at me. I was hoping it was a joke. I almost started to smile when he pulled back and I saw it coming out of my stomach. I was horrified, in shock.

I looked over at my daughter. A little line of blood ran down her rib cage. She laid there dead, looking at me.

I blacked out I don't know how many times. I remembered a

little bit here and there.

"And to think, you were my best friend," he said. "Now that's power."

That's when BMW said, "I wish you could have joined us. I really liked you."

But had I known they were gonna kill my daughter, I wouldn't have hesitated to join 'em. But my fear of living was less than my fear of watching somebody murder somebody.

The old woman said, "You got over your fear when you stood up for what was right, not when you became a killer. You're not empowered at all. That's Nina talking," she said. "She's all in your head."

But why did she have to die?

We were gonna bring the whole organization down, me and the old lady. But she was right. I had gained my courage when I was able to stand up to Nina. She's the one that ruled my heart. She built me up and crushed me at the same time. She filled me up and left me wanting, a hunger, a thirst that would not and could not be quenched.

I stood over her body many nights as she slept. She was a picture of unfathomable beauty. Killer. I wasn't a killer. I was a coward. And she ruled over me like I was a puppy.

"Sit."

"Roll over."

"Beg now."

"Thatta boy."

"Good boy."

"I'm not your puppy, Nina. I could never marry you."

"Marry me, honey? You would never ask me, in fear of rejection. Afraid that I would tell you no. But the secret is, you want me to be yours, your wife, more than anything in the world."

"That's a lie, Nina."

"I'm marrying Delie."

"You'll never marry her. Not as long as I'm alive."

But she was right. No matter how much I denied it, I was in love with her. But I knew I could never ask her to marry me, just like she said. She had a way of rejecting me and making me like it. The more she stayed at the house, the less sleep I got."

"Must you be so conservative? You don't have to recycle everything."

Delie stood over the garbage can, picking out plastic.

"Rich people don't do that, you know."

"Just helping with the environment," she said. "We've all got to do our part."

I told her, "I wouldn't want my wife digging through garbage like that."

She looked up at me. "Well maybe it's a good thing I'm not your wife then."

I came over, bent over, picked up a plastic bottle out of the garbage, and smiled at her as I looked at her. "Maybe you're right."

She said, "Ah, don't give up so easy now. Maybe a wife is just what you need."

We both stood up to our feet. "Is it?"

She looked at me sternly, took the bottle out of my hand, and threw it back in the garbage can. "You need empowerment," she said.

"Again with that? I'm standing here pouring out my heart to you."

But she didn't love me.

Not like she pretended she did.

Fourth part of the initiation. Find the next victim. Twelve members. Twelve parts. Every member that moved up moved out. Everything from getting rid of the body down to new recruits. Every month, twelve more, and then twelve more, and then so on, and so on.

But I had five of 'em left.

"We couldn't even clean the body up," the sheriff said. "Radiovac came in. The whole house was contaminated with radiation. They had to dig the whole house up, body and all. They had to dig the whole place up, twenty feet deep. Six hundred thousand dollars it took to destroy that house and get rid of it. Six hundred thousand dollars of contamination."

But I knew the young arrogant sucker. He put three hundred million in it the first year. By the third year, he had already put four or five hundred more million in it. It was layered in gold, silver. It was all contaminated.

I put the bullets on the table. "I only used one. Here are the five back. You keep the money I owe you. You take these. I don't care what you do with 'em. I need my regular bullets."

He looked at me at first. "A deal's a deal, man. You've had my bullets for a month. I could've sold 'em a month ago."

"You keep the bullets. I'll give you your three grand."

"Nah man, I need it now."

"I'll give it to you next month. You sell the bullets between now and then, get your money out of 'em, plus you'll still get my three thousand."

He picked the bullets up, put 'em in his pocket, and started to walk away.

"Hey!"

He turned around abruptly and sternly looked at me.

"What about my bullets?" I asked.

He took two cases out of his pocket and put 'em up on the table. "These are on the house 'til next month."

He was about to get on my bad side, but my quarrel wasn't with him. There was always gonna be guns, and there was always gonna be gun dealers. Just don't get caught in between the two. Those that do, they end up on the six o'clock news. Or on a coroner's table being examined for the cause of death.

———————————

"But I'm a killer," the western said.

"I can't go back to town now," the gun fighter said.

My favorite part.

"I can't go back to town now."

It was a rough ride in that motor boat.

"What's in the newspaper, old woman?"

174

"Them's fish for the fish market, young man."

"We're quite a pair, ain't we? An old woman, a young man."

"Ain't we though?" She smiled without those teeth and squinted her old eyes because the sun was bright that day.

There were small white tops. So the water was quite choppy, and the boat was quite small. After about twenty minutes, my ankles began to throb. I would have to get them looked at immediately.

That's when I saw the head master heading into an office. "Dr. Aldan Lawrence," it said on the door. It must have been his family doctor, but next to the building was another doctor. Foot and Ankle Doctor, a bone doctor. "Hmmm." I thought I would kill two birds with one stone.

When I walked in, I didn't wait very long before the doctor came in. He told me his name. I said, "Yeah, Doc, that's all good. What can you do for this?"

I raised up my pants leg. He bent down, touched where my bones were crooked, and said, "This will have to be broken again."

"How long will I be down?"

"I can probably have you up and walking the same day. I'll have to drill some pins in, set the bone. We have bone glue. You don't have to wait for it to mend."

"Then what's the pin for?"

"That's to hold it in place because after we close the skin up, it takes four hours for it to set."

"And then?"

"Well then, Mr. Hourson, you'll be out walking in no time."

"On both feet?"

"Yes, but there is a little catch. It's sixteen thousand dollars per foot."

"That's a little steep."

"Yes, I'm afraid it is. But you come back when you get some insurance and I'll be glad to do the operation for you."

"I need it done now. Here's forty thousand dollars." I laid out the cash.

"Well, I can't do it right—"

I said, "Right now. I need it done right this minute."

He looked at the money. "We'll have to go over to the hospital."

"What hospital?"

He told me the name. "I'll meet you over there," I said, and then I left.

I woke up in recovery. "It's been four hours, Mr. Hourson. Let's see if we can get you up on your feet."

"What?!? What did you say?"

"The surgery was a success."

I had bandages on my feet, well, on my ankles.

"I used butterfly stitches so you won't have to have the stitches taken out. As soon as you're able to get dressed, you're welcome to leave."

I was starting to get my emotions about me when I stood up on my feet and my ankles did not hurt.

"Now you've got a certain amount of painkiller in you, and that will wear off in a few hours. But here's a prescription, just in case you need it, but you probably won't."

But I did. For the next three weeks, I sat around in the car that I had purchased for one hundred dollars. It was a teenage kid. It was before my operation. I was walking up the road, well onto my journey of killing, and as I walked up the road, I saw the car in the middle of the road. He had tried to crank it for the last time. When I got up to the car, I was still on the sidewalk when he stepped out of the car.

"Hey mister! You wanna buy a car?"

I said, "I'll give you one hundred dollars for it."

"Deal!"

"Does it run?"

"If it's got gas, it runs."

"Why don't you put gas in it then?"

"Cause I ain't got no money. I was on my way outta town. I'm gonna hitchhike."

He pulled out the title and signed it over to me. I went and got some gas. After I paid him, he was long on his way, gone completely outta sight. I got a pretty good deal for a hundred bucks. I kept that car the whole time I was alive.

Chapter 18
The Curse - Revenge

"Revenge," the old woman kept saying, over and over again. Echoing, over again. "It's cruel as the grave. That's in the Bible, you know."

"You know, I don't even know your name."

"You can just call me old woman."

"Okay, old woman, what's your name?"

"Well, if you must know. It's Mildred."

"Well, that's my grandma's name."

"I bet she was a tough old bird."

"Not really, she was just as scared as I was, stayed in the house all the time, scared to death to do anything, so she never did anything. Ever. Never did anything," I told the old woman.

"That's a hard rule to live by," she said. "Maybe you oughta change your ways."

"But how? My grandma raised me. My momma and daddy died long ago."

"Fear's kept me alive," I said, "and it ain't like I'm afraid. I just don't like getting hurt when I do things."

Like burning down your house?

You never told me that, Grandma.

That you were the one that set the fire that killed Momma and Daddy. She died soon after that, but she took the truth to the grave. The truth that she would never tell me. Yeah, I found out.

But that ain't like murder, is it? Yeah, she was negligent. It was written all over her face, but I didn't know it then. But I've learned to read people since then, and looking back, she was guilty. She knew she was. But me knowing was more than she could handle. She could no longer look me in the face.

"You've got to be the saddest person on the face of this Earth," the old woman said. "If you ask me, I think your whole life is pathetic."

I looked down and said, "I'm pathetic."

"Scared of your own shadow, never standing up for yourself," she murmured.

But I did stand up to 'em.

That's the reason they killed me.

That's the reason Nina killed me.

A thousand times she killed me.

With every breath I took.

She stayed at the house more and more, coming in between me and my fiance who I had not yet proposed to. It was for the best. I was better off dead.

Empowerment, yeah, you're empowered alright. Once you kill someone, the feeling of it never goes away. The softness you once had dwindles away each day, and the cowardness, the fear of the dark.

The fear of living.

The fear of dying.

The fear itself disappears.

I wouldn't even stick my foot out from under the covers in the dark at night, for God's sake, but now I could crawl through a man hole, jump out of a plane. I could scuba dive, mountain climb. I wasn't afraid of nothing.

But every one of them, tragic deaths.

The curse of the dagger.

It was long and skinny like a screw driver. Like a bayonet. The only thing sharp was the squared off end. It had no cutting edge at all. It was dull pointed like a screwdriver. So when you pushed it in, it didn't cut. It ripped, causing even more pain. It was a horrible device.

The handle weaved through the center of both sides with some kind of cord turned to metal after it was weaved. Looking at it, it hardly looked scary, but after observing it closely, especially with it going in right beneath your center rib cage, it becomes horrifying.

The look of pleasure on her face while she killed me. It was like a new high for her. But even with my last heart beat, my last drop of blood going through my heart as I faded off, I couldn't help but to think how beautiful she was and how much I still loved her as the tears rolled down past my temple into my hairline.

She kissed my dead body and got off the top of me. "That wasn't as easy as I thought it would be," she said, not feeling the empowerment like she thought she ought to have. Instead, she felt empty, cold, deserted, and the worst part, she felt all alone for the first time. She could still see my face, even when she turned her head away. "I love you, Nina."

That's when she turned back and looked at me, and for the first the first time in her life meant what she said when she said, "I love you, too. I'm already missing you."

She looked down at the dagger, still unclothed, and pulled it between her cleavage. The blood was still dripping as it got on her chest, and a big smile came across her face.

But she didn't feel the empowerment.

She didn't feel the power.

She just felt the need to kill again.

And again. And again.

But the head master was right. Nina wasn't right. But she was extraordinary.

She put her clothes on and looked at my dead body. "You being alive was a surprise. But you coming back, killing all those people that you loved so dearly, made you my top prize. Nobody's killed that many people that they cared about. Especially not me," she said.

She closed the door on her way out, carefully planning her little schemes. But when she was being killed, what was being said and what she was hearing was totally different from what really happened. She thought it was me. She called me by name. She was delirious. She knew her time had come, and she knew what she had done to me. But now, it was payback time.

"I love you, Nina," I said. "Almost as much as you love me."

The dagger was only a half inch deep when she began to scream, "I love you, too."

And then another half inch, very slowly.

But when it got an inch and a half to two inches deep, she sobered right up when she woke up and he was saying, "I love you, Nina."

Her latest seduction.

Her would be victim became her demise.

Her would be lover became her killer.

But before she closed her eyes, she saw me again on top of her as she faded away and said, "I love you, too," calling me by my name."

So even in death, and without even meaning to, I got my revenge.

"Once the killing stops," the old woman said, "everybody involved. If you don't have feelings then, it won't be like me, get on with your life. You'll be destitute, whatever drives you on. "

But it was Nina that drove me on, to the very end.

Killer.

Yes, I was a killer.

But she was a raging psychopath on the inside and a convincing angel on the outside. Killer, not in the least. She was a nympho homicidal maniac. Murderer.

But me, any time my name was mentioned afterward, "Killer," they would say. "He was a killer."

———————

That's when the deputy closed the book and the folders. "Mr.

Hourson. Killer."

The new deputy looked at the sheriff. "Sheriff, that's got to be the saddest man I ever heard about."

His full grown son walked in, the new deputy. "He saved his life, you know. He saved my life, too."

"Yeah, you told me that part. Sheriff, I'm telling you, it's just the craziest story I ever heard."

KILLER

And at the same time, the old man took his mask off. The old woman never died. Mildred.

www.ingramcontent.com/pod-product-compliance
Lightning Source LLC
Chambersburg PA
CBHW060745180626
46818CB00002B/455